P9-CAX-730

TERROR TRAIN

The SS guy wasn't aware of the green-eyed invader until he topped the last rung of his ladder. It was his tough luck. The Hangman exploded a roundhouse kick off the side of the neo-Nazi's head. Sailing off the train, the guy followed his assault rifle and SS cap down into the ravine.

Now Hangman unleashed his Uzi on the Nazis below him. Two guys looked up; two faces were obliterated by 9mm slugs burping from the SMG's snout. Triggering the Israeli subgun one-handed, he stitched a neo-Nazi up the spine and opened the back of the Fourth Reicher's skull with the gory end of his barrage. Bloody chunks of bone and brain followed the dead man off the train...

Other Books in Avon's
KILLSQUAD Series

(#1) COUNTER ATTACK
(#2) MISSION REVENGE

Coming Soon

(#4) THE JUDAS SOLDIERS

Avon Books are available at special quantity discounts for bulk purchases for sales promotions, premiums, fund raising or educational use. Special books, or book excerpts, can also be created to fit specific needs.

For details write or telephone the office of the Director of Special Markets, Avon Books, Dept. FP, 1790 Broadway, New York, New York 10019, 212-399-1357.

KILLSQUAD

#3

LETHAL ASSAULT

FRANK GARRETT

AVON
PUBLISHERS OF BARD, CAMELOT, DISCUS AND FLARE BOOKS

KILLSQUAD #3: LETHAL ASSAULT is an original publication of Avon Books. This work has never before appeared in book form. This work is a novel. Any similarity to actual persons or events is purely coincidental.

AVON BOOKS
A division of
The Hearst Corporation
1790 Broadway
New York, New York 10019

Copyright © 1986 by Dan Schmidt
Published by arrangement with the author
Produced in cooperation with Taneycomo Productions, Inc., Branson, Missouri
Library of Congress Catalog Card Number: 86-90975
ISBN: 0-380-75153-4

All rights reserved, which includes the right to reproduce this book or portions thereof in any form whatsoever except as provided by the U.S. Copyright Law. For information address Taneycomo Productions, Inc., P.O. Box 1069, Branson, Missouri 65616.

First Avon Printing: December 1986

AVON TRADEMARK REG. U.S. PAT. OFF. AND IN OTHER COUNTRIES, MARCA REGISTRADA, HECHO EN U.S.A.

Printed in the U.S.A.

K-R 10 9 8 7 6 5 4 3 2 1

For Tommy and David;
to our mutual key-holding buddy, BB.
What a nightmare.

LETHAL ASSAULT

PROLOGUE

The sound sent a sliver of ice down his spine. At first, Father James McMillan felt fear as he stepped out of his large mud-and-branch frame hut. The whapping bleat, a sound like a swarm of locusts descending to ravage crops, seemed to come from the northeast. Whatever approached the isolated Catholic mission was hidden from the priest's sight by the lush green treeline along the Congo River.

But the sound grew into a humming whine. A familiar sound, Father McMillan thought. Growing. Looming. A sound of terror coming, the priest knew, and he felt his fear edge toward panic. A sound that seemed to shake the swampy shores of the lower Congo. A sound that seemed to slowly split asunder the gray jungle sky of dawn.

Panic then seized Father McMillan. His mind screamed at him, *It can't be. God, no!*

Not now, he told himself. Not now, he implored of his Maker. Not after all the work the Saint Joseph's Relief Program has done to save the Lulua, Bakongo, Bateke, and Bangalas tribes of the Congo. The famine that they had ended. The dreaded malaria, yellow fever, yaws, dysentery, and sleeping sickness that they had cured. The barbaric tribal customs, the mutilation and disfigurement of flesh, the cannibalism the natives had practiced, all of which had been replaced with Christianity.

But lately Father McMillan had heard the tales from other tribesmen, the *ju-ju* men. He had dismissed, or pointedly ignored, those stories. He had done so out of fear. The Belgian Congo, he knew, had seen enough horror since Belgium granted the country its independence in 1960. Still, how many villages had been razed by marauding tribes and soldiers since then? How many brutal men had risen to dictatorship only to be assassinated by men more ruthless than they since that day of so-called independence? How many military coups? How much bloodshed must bathe the Congo, he wondered, before there was peace?

Something twisted at Father McMillan's guts as he saw the Luluans step from their huts, look up at the sky, point toward the river. Something warned the priest that the spirit of kindness and compassion would not save them any longer from the strife that had long afflicted the rest of the country.

"Dytaka yimht ubana! Dytaka yimht ubana!"

The white death squads, McMillan heard the Luluans say in their native tongue. *The great birds that bring fire and death from the skies.*

McMillan froze in the center of the village. He sensed the mounting panic of the villagers. Fear became a palpable force around him.

Villagers frantically chattered on. A cluster of Luluan boys on the village outskirts stopped mashing the grass they would use to bait fish traps later on in the morning. A dozen nuns dressed in blue-and-white habits stepped out of the quarters at the far end of the village, stood on the steps for a moment, then quickly strode toward the source of the commotion.

The river treeline wavered like fields of wheat in the breeze. Wind then gusted and funneled dust sheets through the Luluan village. A second later, Father McMillan saw them.

And his worst fear became reality.

Four black helicopter gunships soared low over the treeline. A red banner with a black swastika was painted on the nose of each gunship. Father McMillan couldn't, didn't believe what he saw. The *ju-ju* men had been right. *Zaanis,* they had called them.

Nazis. But how? Father McMillan heard his mind scream. It was a plot, he thought, by the apartheid regime in South Africa. The racist poison had spread from the Republic, come to plague the Congo missions.

But the priest had no time to rationalize this horror. A nightmare, a living hell from one of the most terrible times in the history of man, had been resurrected. The black gunships with the swastikas, he knew, would spare no one and nothing.

The Luluans scattered as the gunships swooped over the huts like giant vultures. Great tongues of fire spewed forth from the silver nozzles attached to the turrets of the gunships. Fire whooshed, roared to life over the brittle, dried-out branch roofs.

"No!" McMillan screamed uselessly at the helicopters as waves of fiery pincers swept over the huts, scissored, and lapped up villagers. "Nooooooo! Not here. Not them!"

Autofire blazed from the open fuselage doors. Mounted M60s cut loose. Human torches danced around the frozen figure of Father McMillan. Bullets zipped up puffs of dust before drilling into the fleeing Luluans.

For a stretched second that felt like an eternity to him, Father McMillan watched in horror as the black-uniformed white men unleashed their hail of death from above. Finally, M60s barking, HK91s blazing over his head, McMillan bolted, sweeping up a child in his arms. In the distance he spotted the tribal chieftain, Nambala, cutting through the curling black tendrils of smoke. Behind Nambala, the sisters of Saint Joseph's moved with frenzied speed to save the children.

Rage contorted the chieftain's features as he pointed a shaking finger in the white priest's direction. "You bring the white demons down upon us! *Dytaka yimht ubana!*"

The priest was about to tell the Luluan chief how wrong he was. But McMillan stumbled, pitching face-first to the ground. The child in his arms suddenly burst like a water balloon. Gore washed over the priest's face. Bile burned into his throat. His mind swam dizzily in this madness. Agonized shrieks lanced his brain. He stared at his crimson-slick hands, paralyzed by terror, then saw villagers pounded by the hailing leadstorms through the walls of fire.

Father McMillan struggled to stand. A furious gust of wind hammered at his back. His legs were like jelly beneath him, and he fell, dust clogging his lungs, choking him.

The gunships landed.

It was a smell that reminded him of Auschwitz. Of the ovens that had consumed thousands of the Jews and Poles. Thousands, *ja,* Alois Schnell thought as he stepped out of the gunship's hull. Thousands had not been enough. There had been survivors of the Holocaust. Too many survivors.

Here, though, on the Dark Continent, it would be different, he vowed to himself. Here, the Thousand Year Reign would be created by himself and his brother, Herbert Schnell. And the vision of their god and hero, *der Führer,* would live on in the glory of the Teutonic people. As it should have been and always would be, he told himself. *Now and forever.*

But first, he thought, the savages had to be dealt with.

Behind the tall, lean, white-haired Schnell, a dozen black-uniformed storm troopers armed with HK91s and Belgium FN-LARs jumped out of the fuselage.

Schnell waved an arm. "Purify this place. Exterminate the vermin."

He felt an instant, delicious jolt of excitement as he watched his *Einsatz* commandos clean up "the garbage of humanity." *Purify*, he thought as the blistering roar of autofire filled the village and the screams ripped through the air. He liked the image of himself as "the Purifier." The Surgeon, as he had been known during the War for the Fatherland, was old and outdated. And that tag tended to remind him of failure.

"Please, please. For the love of God!"

It was the priest. Schnell felt a depthless loathing overwhelm him as he stepped toward the Catholic missionaries that his men were now rounding up. They were foolish, pigheaded whites, he thought, waving a banner of righteousness in a land of savagery and ignorance. They had come with their false words of a false God. They had come with their bleeding hearts full of false pride, their eyes wet with the blind stupidity of the white man's guilt. They had come to civilize the inferiors. They were nothing but a disgrace. They deserved death, Alois Schnell knew, before the purer strain of the Master Race was contaminated, weekened. For many inferior whites, he thought, Africa would indeed become the white man's grave.

His hands clasping a riding crop behind his back, Herbert Schnell strode to catch up to his brother beyond the ring of gunships. Like his older brother, Herbert Schnell was tall, lean, his hair white and closely cropped. But unlike the fire that burned in Alois Schnell's blue eyes, there was a haunted, pained look in the younger Schnell's pale blue orbs.

And even though he was several years younger than his brother, the spiderweb lines that criss-crossed his long, guant face made Herbert Schnell look more than a decade older than Alois. A monocle covered Herbert Schnell's left eye.

The brothers converged in the center of the village. There they stood, spectators to the massacre. The black-uniformed commandos ran down the surviving Luluans with blazing assault rifles. Nuns attempted to shield the children from death, but they were also shredded to bloody rags by autofire. Other neo-Nazis hauled in the nuns and Nambala. The storm troopers dragged and kicked their captives along. Several of the white invaders laughed. Alois Schnell, breathing in the pungent stench of roasting flesh, ordered the summary executions of all surviving Luluans except for Nambala. He had plans for the black Lulua chieftain.

As gunfire sounded, Schnell looked at the village —the black bodies torn and twisted in death, the huts crumbling to the ground. Shock invasions had always worked so perfectly for the Germans. Perfect planning and swift and brutal execution had been the key to the Third Reich's short-lived conquest of much of Europe.

A smile slashing his thin, bloodless lips, Alois looked at Herbert. His brother returned the smile. Herbert understood. Words were often empty vessels, Alois Schnell knew. Only action truly spoke, he believed. Progress and civilization were nearly upon the Dark Continent. Key government officials high up in the white-controlled apartheid "Brit Colony" of South Africa had been bought and sold. A handful of very important Boers, too. Thanks, he knew, to the pirated fortunes of Third Reich gold and diamonds. And, of course, a mutual, undying belief in the supreme destiny of the white race.

Schnell looked at his commandos. "Take them," he said in a weary-sounding voice, jerking a nod at McMillan, Nambala, and the surviving nuns.

"Why?" the priest pleaded. "Why are you do-ing—"

An *Einsatz* commando chopped McMillan over the head with the butt of his FN-LAR, dropping the priest to his knees.

With a feeling of deep pride, Alois Schnell watched as his troops hustled the prisoners toward the gunships. He had selected the best soldiers from the South African Army and police. Outcasts and renegades from BOSS and SAP—malcontents and dogs of war, he knew, most without the first drop of Teutonic blood. But they would have to do. They were efficient. They were well trained. They followed orders.

And they believed.

Alois Schnell met McMillan's terrified gaze as his commandos dragged the priest by him.

"Where is your God now?" the Surgeon spat, his ice-blue eyes like two chips of Arctic stone. "Your pleas fall on deaf ears. This God of yours has forsa-ken you, *scheisskopf.*" He laughed. "Your God is dead."

The two brothers lingered while the storm troopers slung the captives into the gunships. Cap-tives, *nein,* Alois Schnell thought. Guinea pigs, *ja.*

Their suffering and eventual deaths, Schnell knew, would serve the Reich well.

The Fourth Reich.

The vision of *Mein Kampf* was soon to be the coming glory of the Master Race. And, Alois Schnell knew, the white man would praise him for his her-oism, for unchaining him from the bonds of the infe-riors who would topple civilization with their savagery and ignorance.

And the white man would also bow down to the masters of the Master Race.

It was Alois Schnell's destiny. A destiny that had been denied him more than forty years ago because of the arrogance of *der Führer.*

The Congo was only the first vessel in the heart

of the Dark Continent. South Africa, he knew, was
ready to fall next.

Together, the Schnells turned away from the
flaming slaughterbed. Together, they strode toward
the gunships, hands clasped behind their backs.

Fire roared into the dawn sky over the Congo.

CHAPTER ONE

The Hangman hated to coin clichés. But if there was such a thing as a human sewer, then every last city along the shores of the Great Lakes was a cesspool created from the anus of mankind. The Motor City, Detroit, was at the top of the industrial dung heap as far as the man from the CIA's Special Operations Division was concerned. As he turned off East Jefferson Avenue along the Detroit River, searching for any spot where he could park his white '59 Corvette convertible, he shook his head in sadness, staring up at the glass-and-concrete monoliths of downtown Motor City. A thick gray blanket hung over the skyline. And it wasn't thunderclouds. *Ah, progress,* the SOD man thought.

Not long ago, he knew, Detroiters had taken modest pride in calling theirs "the most beautiful city in America." But since post—World War II, Detroit had rolled up its sleeves. Old Georgian mansions along Woodward and Jefferson avenues were converted into rooming houses. Trees had been chopped down

9

by the hundreds so that streets could be widened.
Snappy little slogans like "Dynamic Detroit"
"Watch Detroit Grow, Better Still Grow With It"
had come down on the Motor City like an anvil,
with the influx of every race and nationality known
to man. With the melting pot and the meteoric rise
of the city as the world's onetime leading automo-
bile manufacturer, though, came the inevitable and
inescapable deluge of all mankind's ills. The price to
be paid for the evolution of technology. Yeah, the
Hangman thought, Detroit now boasted more than
seven thousand factories. The Detroit River, which
connected lakes Huron and Erie, was a vital link to
the Great Lakes. And the Saint Lawrence River
water route was supposedly the busiest in the
world. *So fucking what?* Hell, these days it wouldn't
take much of a miracle for a man to walk across the
gummy, sludge-slick surface of Lake Erie or Michigan. And his name wouldn't have to be Jesus.

Worse still for the big boys in their executive
suites and the labor force down in the factories,
three-fifths of the world's automobiles were no
longer made in Michigan. The industrial samurai of
the "Rising Sun" had seen to that. Huge factory
layoffs in the Motor City, tough overseas competi-
tion, and the demand for a small economic car had
cut the balls off of the once mighty Detroit. Yeah, he
thought, there was always a sign on Easy Street—
be prepared to come to a screeching halt.

Crime. Pollution. Urban decay. These days, that
was what the Motor City boasted. And it wasn't
likely that things were going to get better anytime
soon.

The Hangman parked his 'Vette on a side street
off East Jefferson. He looked at a row of tenement
dwellings, brick bulkheads smudging a dirty gray
sky. Blacks roamed their neighborhood streets at
that early-morning hour. Trash mounds lined the
gutters. A baby squalled from somewhere.

It wasn't the best place in the city to park a vintage car, hell no. But it was available, and the Hangman didn't have all day to comb the streets for a space.

No sooner had the Hangman stepped out of his 'Vette when three of the city's finer citizens approached him. The SOD man assumed that the three grim-faced, mean-eyed blacks strolling up the sidewalk toward him weren't a welcoming committee. And the Hangman hadn't seen flashier threads since *Super Fly*.

The Hangman figured that politeness was possibly in order. "How you fellas doing today?"

The black hulk in the middle turned to one of his brothers and sneered. No, Hangman thought, politeness was out.

The trio of urban beauties stepped right up to the lone white man as he moved onto the sidewalk. What the three black punks thought they saw was one lone honky cat ripe for a pick. What they ended up seeing instead was Super Honky. And instead of an easy mugging, what they ended up with was a quick trip to the city morgue and a one-way ticket to the Great Panther Rally in Hell.

It was over within a split second after one of the citizens growled, "You gonna park here, lez see sum bread, white muthafucker."

Personally, the CIA specialist had nothing against blacks or any minorities. *They were all God's beautiful children, right?* he thought. Then a switchblade snapped open in the hand of a punk. Beauty went straight into the eye of the beholder. And the Hangman felt more than a little pleasure as he sent these three to Satan's garbage heap, the dung pile of the bleeding hearts.

Hangman took out the punk with the switchblade first. A lightning spearhand, two fingers through the punk's eyeballs and into the brain. It was a little messy, yeah. *But a little lovin', touchin', squeezin',* Super Honky thought, *went a long way.*

The next urban beauty found his nuts driven up into his stomach with a snap-knee kick.

"Dirty pool, huh?" the Hangman rasped, thinking, *That one's for you, Teddy, babe, you macho-stud killer of pregnant women, you....*

For shock effect, the Hangman ripped the last punk's ear off with a claw hand. He handed the piece of bloody meat to the black, thinking, *How you doing there, Jesse, you big, beautiful Reverend in Christ Jesus.* Then he finished the punk with a knife-edged hand to his throat, crushing the black's neck. No, the Hangman thought, casual killing just wasn't his bag.

The black punk whose nuts had been turned to powder slumped to his knees, clutching at his punished groin. Vomit dribbled from his gaping mouth. He whimpered, gasping for air. The Hangman ended those pitiful cries, splintering his last victim's temple with the knuckles of one hand. The deathblow rearranged the punk's Afro. Super Fly the Stud became Super Sack of Shit. These guys, Hangman thought, probably jacked off on subway trains when they weren't beating up little old ladies.

Detroit was now minus three possible candidates for mayor.

The Hangman turned away from the kill-zone. Quickly, he put distance between himself and his latest urban renewal project. There was indeed beauty, he decided, even in ugliness.

The Hangman admitted he felt a little angry that day, but things were just starting to heat up along the Detroit River. Perhaps, he thought, the killing had only started.

Several more blocks passed underfoot, and the Renaissance Center loomed into view. Beyond the circular seventy-three-story hotel and the four thirty-nine-story office buildings of the Center, the Hangman saw the veil of black smoke that curtained the eastern horizon, as factory stacks belched burning waste and freighters chugged down the river.

It had taken long hours of plowing through Intelligence dossiers and tracking down leads in Chicago, Milwaukee, and Gary before the Hangman found the hydra's head of Merlmann Allied Chemicals, Inc., here. The Merlmann office was located in the penthouse suite on the thirty-ninth floor of one of the four Renaissance office buildings. Merlmann Allied Chemicals was a major distributor of chemicals that treated industrial and toxic wastes. It was only a front, the Hangman knew, for a much larger black-market operation. An operation that dealt in arms exports to right-wing terrorist groups in South Africa. Those exports included nerve gas, the disassembled parts of helicopter gunships, and possibly biological and nuclear warfare. Something hot, the Hangman knew, was boiling on the Dark Continent.

The Hangman intended to find out what it was.

Hangman walked into the receptionist's bay area. Plaques picturing guys with toothy grins lined the white walls of Merlmann. Guys shaking hands and receiving awards from hotshot military brass and chubby, apple-cheeked politicos. Most of whom, the Hangman thought, striding toward a blond receptionist with tits that threatened to bust out of her white blouse, were butt-fucking the taxpayers.

"Can I help you, sir?" the blond asked the Hangman.

The blond froze, staring at the SOD man in the black leather flight jacket for a long moment. What she saw was a pair of green eyes that glinted like snakeskin from behind hooded lids. Eyes that looked as if they belonged more to some reptile than to a human being. And a long, gaunt, square-jawed face that could have been carved from some voodoo death mask.

The Hangman glimpsed his reflection in the wall

mirror behind the receptionist. Christ, he was looking old and ugly, he thought. Living on the edge of
Hell, he knew, had a way of doing that. Somehow
the fake scar, mustache, and beard accentuated his
cryptic mask. Dyed coal-black hair completed his
disguise.

"I'm Peter Stein," the Hangman said. "I'm with
one of the sister companies out of Munich. Mr.
Merlmann is expecting me."

The receptionist went over a ledger on her desk.
"I'm sorry, Mr. Stein, but Mr. Merlmann's schedule
doesn't show your name here."

"It probably wouldn't, Miss. I'm a major stock-
holder in the company. Mr. Merlmann likes to keep
his dealings with investors confidential, you understand."

The blond looked flustered. "Well, he's in a meeting right now."

The Hangman was tired of bullshitting around.
"Yeah, I know all about that meeting" was his parting shot. Swiftly, he moved away from the receptionist area, heading down a long corridor. At the
end of the corridor, he saw the gold plaque with
HAROLD MERLMANN, PRESIDENT hung on one
of the large mahogany double doors.

"Sir. Sir!" the receptionist called out.

The Hangman ignored the blond. Unzipping his
jacket, he opened the door to Merlmann's office. Inside, the four men at the private meeting turned
anxious, angry expressions toward the intruder in
the doorway and froze.

The short, balding Merlmann punched a button
on his desk's intercom, cutting off the receptionist's
voice. The rolls of fat that folded over his belt
buckle made it difficult for Merlmann to move.
"Who the hell do you think you are, barging in here
like this, Mister?" he demanded.

Hangman closed the door behind him. He
glanced at the big black-haired gorilla seated in a
chair to his far left. There were three other guys

seated in wing chairs around Merlmann's massive desk, but they weren't lackey muscle. Recalling the Intelligence photos and dossiers on Harold Merlmann and Associates, the specialist felt as if he personally knew every man there. Present were an Army-Intelligence colonel named Brett Dugan; a major industrial supplies exporter, Alfred Tennebaum; and a corporate lawyer, Benjamin Maximillian. The Hangman read them all as slime. Very dangerous slime. And what they sold was death. None of the slime present, with the exception of the lawyer, appeared concerned about the intrusion. The Hangman and the lawyer locked gazes for a second. That guy had all the legal angles covered for Merlmann, Hangman knew. As a rule of thumb, the Hangman put lawyers one cut below child sodomizers. Someone, the SOD man briefly recalled, had once told him that he had a problem with stereotyping people. He believed that someone had been one of those NOW types. A real dyke women's-libber, he remembered, with a horse's-ass face that would have killed any hard-on instantly.

"I'll ask you once more what you're doing here,. mister, before I call security."

Hangman strode across the room. He pulled out a "business card" and flipped it down on the desk in front of Merlmann.

The fat mogul glanced at the card and growled, "Peter Stein. Free-lancer. Just what do you free-lance, mister?"

The Hangman showed Merlmann and the other pillars of the community a graveyard smile. "Death."

Anger blazed in Merlmann's eyes. He looked at the gorilla. "Throw him out of here."

Hangman took a step back and turned slightly as the gorilla lumbered toward him. "Sit tight, pal. I'm not finished."

The gorilla didn't listen.

The guy found he was minus a workable kneecap. After that lightning downward kick, the Hangman knocked out every one of the gorilla's front teeth with a backhand hammerfist. Just to show Merlmann and his buddies that he'd gotten up on the wrong side of the bed.

They believed it.

Gorilla-boy hit the floor with a thud. Groaning, he spat out splintered pieces of teeth along with a steady flow of blood.

Merlmann reached for the intercom.

A Walther PPK/S .380 ACP snaked from inside the Hangman's jacket. The SOD man broke the ice further. The Hangman's favored field handgun piece, the *Polizei Pistole, Kriminal,* spat out a silenced W-W Silvertip hollow-point man-stopper. The renegade colonel found he had a third, and very unwanted, eye in the middle of his forehead. Brett Dugan hit the plush brown carpet on his back, knocked out of the black-market arms picture for good. Kill one, get the attention of all, the Hangman thought. Yeah, he knew, it had always worked for Joey Stalin. There were lessons to be learned from history. Even from the great butchers of history. Particularly when those lessons could be applied to other butchers.

Alfred Tennebaum gasped. The Hangman drilled a .380 ACP round through that vented maw, blasting Tennebaum's breath out of the back of his neck with a W-W Silvertip ventilator. One black-market exporter became an import to Hell.

Merlmann froze in horror.

The lawyer wobbled to his feet. He held his hands up in front of his Gucci suit jacket. He shook like a pissed-on leaf. "Please, I—I don't kno-know who you are...but, can't w-we talk this out...like reasonable men?"

The Hangman almost laughed. Instead, he tore the throat out of the corporate big shot with a .380 ACP hellion.

The Hangman turned the Walther on the fat mogul. "Where has all the love gone in the world, huh, Merlmann?"

"Wh-what?" Merlmann croaked.

"If you want to stay in the land of the living, you'd better answer some questions."

Merlmann hesitated, then his hand streaked for the intercom. A silenced .380 ACP drilled a ragged hole through that hand. Before Merlmann could scream, the Hangman shot his arm out and grabbed the black-market arms dealer by his jacket lapel. Furious, the specialist hauled Merlmann over the top of his desk, sweeping leather pencil holders, intercom, and family portraits off the desktop with the fat mogul's body. Hangman dumped Merlmann on the floor and rammed the Walther's silencer against the bridge of the dirty mogul's nose. Maximillian's lifeless eyes stared, inches from Merlmann's twitching lips.

"Let's cut the bullshit, Merlmann. I'm not some choirboy at your church. I know who and what you are. And I know some very lethal, very black shipments have been going regularly to Cape Town and Durban. Shipments like nerve gas, Huey gunship parts, small and large arms, and even a shipment of uranium and plutonium. Tell me about it."

"Wh-who are you? CIA?"

Hangman knelt down on Merlmann's injured hand. "IRS, fat man," he rasped as Merlmann cried out in pain.

"All right . . . listen . . . I—I don't really know who the principal purchasers are—"

Hangman pressed down on Merlmann's hand with his knee and slapped his hand over the mogul's mouth to silence the cry of pain. "Try again."

Merlmann injected defiant hatred into Hangman's eyes. "I just fill the orders."

"From whom? You don't just fill a ten-million-dollar arms order and not know who you're dealing with, Merlmann."

"There's a purchasing agent in Cape Town, but he's only a middleman. The orders are broken down by someone in the Bureau of State Security. Then spread out across South Africa. Pretoria. Johannesburg. The Transvaal. Bloemfontein. Shipments go in as industrial machinery. I've never gotten the names of any purchasers on the other end, I swear it. But I can tell you the shipments end up in Central Africa."

"The Belgian Congo?"

"Zaire," Merlmann corrected.

"Whatever," the Hangman growled. Hell, he knew the Belgian Congo had been renamed Zaire after Joseph Desire Mobutu seized control of the government following the Katanga secession movement, the rebellion that was ended by so-called UN troops. The Katanga rebels were then forced to flee to neighboring Angola. There, they set up their Marxist shop once again. Christ, the Hangman thought, those Marxist African countries changed names with every other military coup and its dictator, and it was a job in itself just to keep those Marxist spear-chucking states straight. The Dark Continent, he knew, was a time bomb for damn sure, set to blow at any time. With or without white colonial control. No matter how bad the black man believed he had it under the colonial thumb of the French, Germans, Brits, Belgians, and Portuguese, he had a living hell on his hands under the hammer and the scythe. Mass murder and mass starvation in those Marxist African countries was a daily way of life. The Hangman knew it from countless, ugly firsthand experiences when on covert CIA operations in Angola, then Rhodesia—now called Zimbabwe. Sure, he admitted, since the first African companies were formed by Elizabeth I, James I, and Charles I, and a permanent British base was established on the Gambia in 1631—beginning the scramble for Africa by the Europeans—the black Africans had been gripped in the hold of false stability that earmarked every successful colony. Sure, the white man in Africa did little to improve native education or living standards, the white man's primary interest being the extraction of plentiful natural resources. And the Belgians had been a prime example of the white rape of Africa. Hell, the Hangman figured, he couldn't answer for anyone's sins but his own. Certainly, he knew, and history had proven, that independence from the so-called "white oppressors"—a term the Soviets had flung at black Africans over and over until they revolted, precipitating a bloodbath from Angola to Uganda during the '60s and '70s—spawned dictatorial regimes that made Nazi Germany look like comic-book chaos. It boiled the Hangman's blood every time he thought about how responsible the fucking yellow-bellied UN had been for the mass chaos and murder that had swept those African countries crying out for independence from the "white oppressors." Never mind, said the overpaid, play-baby bullshitters on the Hill who sought reelection in place of reality, that the UN had turned over Angola, Zambia, Somalia, Mozambique, Ethiopia, and Zaire to one-party dictatorships. All of them were black countries, where a few fat cats rode around in new Mercedes while the masses groveled to eat elephant or buzzard shit. Or each other. The fucking United Nations, the Hangman thought. UN. *Useless Numbnuts.*

"You must have some idea who the purchasers on the other end in the Belgian Congo are, fat man," the Hangman growled. "If you can't come up with anything better than that, kiss your ass bye-bye."

"L-look, I can't tell you much, I swear to God... Zaire...the purchasers are there...Nazis, I think. War criminals."

"Nazis?"

"Last week," Merlmann blurted, "my sellers hit two Jewish agents from West Germany's Center for

Nazi War Criminals in Cape Town. The Jews were on to our buyers."

"Why?"

"Be-because...they seemed to think there's a conspiracy somewhere within the South African apartheid government. The Jews thought the arms went deep in the Congo—Zaire—to a military base. A Fourth Reich military base."

The Hangman looked away from Merlmann for a moment. Okay, he thought, according to Intelligence, several Catholic missions in the Congo had been torched in the past month, every villager dead or scattered to the jungle. Why those hits were made, and who were behind them, no one knew. The central government of Mobutu—or, Hangman thought, as the fucker now liked to be called, Mobutu Sese Seko—had been silent on the matter. Yeah, the Hangman knew Zaire supported the Camp David accords and U.S. mediation efforts in South Africa. But Zaire also had an awful lot of cobalt and other raw materials that Uncle Sam, the West, and Russia were licking their lips for. It was one dirty hand washing the other dirty hand there.

The Hangman looked at Merlmann's twisted mask of agony. It was time to end his solo assignment. He had a lot of info to chew over on the way back to the New Mexico base, where Killsquad waited. A war machine, he knew, that was ready to crank it up into high gear once again.

Damn, he thought, the Fourth Reich in Africa. What in the hell were he and his six condemned soliders getting ready to step into now?

"L-listen...I've told you all I know....Jesus, I'm in pain."

The Hangman's green eyes glittered with ice. He stood, aimed the Walther down at Merlmann's face. "Not anymore, fat man."

"No," Merlmann pleaded. "You promised...you said—"

The Walther chugged once. A .380 death message

punched through Merlmann's forehead, ending the fat mogul's squirming.

"You never were in the land of the living," the Hangman said.

The SOD man holstered his Walther. As he headed across the large suite, the gorilla clambered to his feet, his toothless mouth snarling horribly.

The Hangman cycloned into a roundhouse kick. The toe of his shoe shattered the gorilla's sphenoid, driving bone splinters into his brain. After the kill, important matters filtered through the Hangman's mind. First, he hoped that his 'Vette wasn't on cinder blocks when he returned to where he'd parked it. His last worry was that the cops would arrest him for the self-defense killings of those three blacks. One call to the Company and those charges would be dropped like a hot potato, he knew.

As he walked to the double doors, Hangman whistled an old Three Dog Night tune. *Jeremiah was a bullfrog,* he sang to himself. Hell, they didn't write tunes like that anymore, he thought. Perhaps because a whole lot of joy had gone out of the world. Hell, *perhaps* nothing, he sadly told himself.

And closed the door on the slaughterbed behind him.

CHAPTER TWO

The Hangman's war machine was assembled in the briefing room by 1540. As the SOD man walked to the front of the room, he sensed the tension in the air, like electrical sparks shooting from severed wires. His six doomed and damned cutthroats sat in desktop chairs spread out in an uneven line before the blackboard and overheard projector. Discipline and conventionality were not their strong points. But then again, Hangman knew he wasn't Frederick the Great or Charlemagne, either. And he wasn't going to kid himself about the kind of human, or inhuman, animals he had on his hands. Six murdering, raping, thieving, bigoted shithead scum had been snatched from the jaws of Death Row at the last moment by his hand for government-sanctioned black operations against international terrorism. And he would treat them all accordingly. Their sins were too many and too ugly for him to deal with the six Death Row soldiers in any way less than brutal.

Hangman glanced at the Damned Six. As usual, the three whites and three blacks sat in two groups, always sticking with their own. But it was their mutual distrust, animosity, fear of each other, and personal prejudices that he had used to fuse them together in one rolling time bomb of a killing machine. And through two suicide search-and-destroy missions, they had cut the hearts right out of monsters that would have devoured thousands of lives.

First the bloody showdown in the Ahaggar Mountains of the Sahara. Razing—with the help of their behemoth helicopter gunship, the UH-1X, Spectre—the Jihad terrorist compound. And of course, he recalled, they had also succeeded with a little help from their Bedouin buddies.

Next, they'd stomped the demon that had been the New Order Church, a fanatical religious organization that had been a front for terrorism against the Continental U.S. Crushed the life out of an egomaniacal tyrant named Eli St. Judas and his outlaw Green Berets, Charlie Company.

That had been a little more than three weeks ago. Plenty of time for the team's war wounds to heal. Since then, the specialist had been planning their next mission, code-named Operation Apocalypse.

Hangman looked over this scurvy, motley crew.

Mac White, the big crew-cut ex-Klansman from Texas. White had worn a white T-shirt to the briefing. On the shirt, in bold black letters, he'd written GEORGE WALLACE FOR PRESIDENT IN '88. A fat wad of chaw pushed White's cheek out. There was a Styrofoam cup on the ex-Klansman's desk. He missed that cup with every other launch of thick, gummy brown juice. *Yeah, a real beautiful human being,* the Hangman thought.

Hangman glanced at Tommy Williams. A black eye patch covered the murderer/bank robber's left eye. A jagged white scar ran down the left side of his face. The disfigurement had come from the wrong end of a switchblade during a rumble with a black gang in Chicago. Williams, the Hangman knew, was one smart-mouth sonofabitch with a chip on his shoulder that not even a wrecking ball could knock off. But the one-eyed pirate—as Williams had become known during the four-year murder and armed-robbery spree across the Midwest and West—was tough, combat-blooded, and always itching for action. Williams also had a problem with graffiti, as the Hangman could see. At the moment, the one-eyed pirate was inscribing some personal expression on his desktop with a Ninja throwing star, a *shuriken*.

Hangman drew a breath and looked next at Lucien Schnell. The big, strapping blond German soldier of fortune was alternately whistling and humming *Deutschland über Alles*. Like any German with pure Teutonic blood flowing in his veins, the Hangman thought, Schnell was always a tall rider on the plains of battle. Schnell had taken those warrior skills across half the globe as a freelance soldier-for-hire. The German also had a problem with sex—he could never get enough. And at a time when he couldn't get enough, Schnell had raped ten young women while traveling across the South and Southwest, pursuing a lead that his Gestapo father and uncle were hiding in the States. Rape, though, hadn't been enough for Schnell. In Schnell's mind, the Hangman believed, the only true consummation of sex ended with him playing the reverse role of the black widow spider.

Hangman turned brief attention to the three blacks chosen. They weren't any prettier, he thought.

Leroy "Lightning Bomber" Walker. The big ex-heavyweight boxer had killed a few people in a fit of rage when his fight career was on the ropes. A meteoric rise to overnight superstardom in the ring had taken its toll on the ghetto warrior from Chicago's South Side. Walker had also worn a white

T-shirt to the briefing. On the shirt he had drawn a clenched black fist blasting through a white brick wall. Beneath the drawing, he'd written the slogan he'd used in the ring—NEVER SAY DIE.

Hangman then raked a look over the last two blacks chosen. Rollo "Ice Pick" Barnes. The hit man from Harlem had been the kingpin of his own Black *Cosa Nostra*. Not even Barnes could recall how many hoods, crooked politicos, and street gunsels he'd taken out with his favorite killing piece: the ice pick. It didn't matter now, the Hangman knew. Barnes was bought and sold. And his soul belong to some ultimate dire fate. Violent death was the only destiny that waited for Barnes at the end of his troubled road. Around his neck, the Harlem assassin wore a large crucifix with a black Jesus on it. Barnes, Hangman noticed, had also worn a white T-shirt to the briefing. On it the hit man from Harlem had drawn an eyeball. Around the eyeball, the Hangman saw a sketching of his own ugly mug. And it wasn't even a bad likeness of himself, the Hangman thought. Beneath the eye, Barnes had written BIG BROTHER LIVES. The Hangman felt the corner of his mouth twist in a crooked grin. He wasn't aware that he had so many Sunday-afternoon artists on his hands. He would have to drop Langley a note, order a few easels.

The only "misfit" in this cutthroat pack was James Jackson. The fisherman from the Florida Coast had been framed for the murders of three federal agents by the drug lords he'd hustled coke and pot for aboard his cabin cruiser, the *Barracuda Renegade*. Jackson was the closest thing in that room to a nice guy. But the Hangman knew where nice guys finished. Dead-last and facedown in the toilet bowl of their niceness. Scratch one nice guy, the Hangman thought. Unlike the others, Jackson wasn't a natural-born killer. But he had learned killing well. Originally, the Hangman had chosen Jackson because he felt the fisherman deserved an-

other shot at life after being railroaded to Death
Row. For that nice-guy bit, the Hangman thought,
he might someday find himself facedown in his own
toilet bowl.

Now, with two missions under their belts, they
had grown in confidence in their own ability as
search-and-destroy killers. Survived suicide operations that nobody in the CIA had given them a
snowball's chance in Hell of surviving. They were
good, yeah, Hangman knew. But he would never tell
them that. The moment he let up on them, the moment he wasn't reminding them all just what kind
of shitheads they were, then it would be one long
anal-dicking. And it would definitely climax with
blood pouring from his slit throat. Yeah, it was a
bridge they would burn without hesitation if he
gave them the chance. But mutiny meant their own
deaths.

It had been his own idea to use Death Row inmates in the CIA's clandestine war against terrorism. Men, he knew, who had nothing to lose.
Because they had nothing left to live for. Unless, of
course, someone shone them a light at the far end of
the tunnel. The Hangman knew that he wasn't that
light. But he could lead the way in this world war
against terrorists. It was a foregone conclusion that
the end of the tunnel was never going to be reached.

Using hardened criminals for covert suicide operations was nothing new. It dated back to World War
II. When the Allies, Hangman thought, realized
they had a whole helluva lot more on their hands
than they could handle in the German war machine. Then, the worst of criminal dregs were
hauled from the stockade and used against the Axis
Powers. They had even made a movie out of it, the
Hangman knew, authentic down to the last detail,
according to history. He made a mental note to drop
Langley another line and order that movie for his
troops. Factor: motivation.

"All right, let's cut the crap," Hangman began.

Schnell's whistling cut the thick silence. The SOD man looked at the German. "Say, uh, Hoffmann von Fallersleben there," he said dryly. "You mind, huh?"

Schnell stopped whistling the German National Anthem and glared for a second at the Hangman.

"Yeah," White growled, squishing a stream of brown spittle that splashed off his cup. "Sergio Mendez you ain't, German."

"How'd your little trip to Detroit go, Sarge?"

The edge in Williams's voice didn't escape Hangman.

"It was an enlightening and spiritually uplifting experience," he remarked, picking up a pointer and moving to the wall map. "I want to tell you people all about it. So shut up and listen." He pointed to Central Africa on the map. "We're going back to Africa, people. This time the Belgian Congo."

"Zaire, man," Jackson corrected.

"Whatever," Hangman said.

"Pardon the interruption there, Cap'n," Mac White called out, "but Africa's just one big fuckin' mess. Hell, it would take a hundred of us a hundred lifetimes to even begin cleaning up the shit in those Commie baboon countries," he said. Walker turned his head sideways, eyeballing the ex-Klansman. "Christ, why can't we just go someplace like Iran and kill some fuckin' *mullahs?* How 'bout Libya? We could round up the fuckin' colonel, fly out over the Gulf of Sidra. Maybe the USS *Nimitz* will be conducting some exercises over this so-called line of death. We'll make the colonel bow down to Mecca, then kick the Arab dungeater out of the gunship, say maybe a good three thousand feet up. Then we can all stand in the doorway and wave down to our boys on the *Nimitz*. Maybe shoot off a few fireworks just to show the troops we kinda like the job they're doing."

His back to his soldiers, Hangman let his head slump. His eyelids started to close, hiding the rising anger he felt.

"I gotta go along with big mouth on this one, Sarge," Williams said. "Black Africa ain't worth a shit. One look at Zimbabwe, where everybody's walking around calling each other *comrade*, will tell you that. Without the whites there running things, those black countries have no economy to barter with. That's straight from that big Intel dossier you slapped together for us there, Sarge. You gonna be all right up there, Sarge?"

Here we go again, the Hangman thought. *Everybody had to get his two fucking cents in.* It had gone like this at both briefings. Inside the wrong heads, it seemed, a little knowledge could be dangerous. He made another mental note. Call *Agronsky and Company,* then *Face the Nation;* see if he could schedule a special guest appearance for these sweethearts full of compassion and understanding for their fellow man. Yeah, he was really looking forward to this operation.

"Let's set the record straight on this, Cap'n," White said, "before we get too far along on this one. Anything worthwhile to ever come out of Africa is due to the white man. Personally, I don't give a shit about a bunch of stinkin' Chad bushmen. I mean, if it weren't for the white guy, those people would still be up in the trees with the baboons. Hell, even with the help of the Europeans those people over there still fell down out of the fucking trees, went straight past the wheel, and jumped into the driver's seat of a Cadillac. They're still countin' on their fingers and toes."

"Horray for King Leopold over there," Jackson grumbled.

White looked at Jackson and growled, "Somethin' crawl up your black ass today, fisherman?"

"Somethin's gonna crawl all over your face in a second, cracker, if you don't shut up," Walker warned.

"Anytime you think you're man enough, Zambian," White shot back. "You remember that big Irish kid with the left hook, don't ya?"

Walker started to rise, but the Hangman rasped, "Shut the fuck up. All of ya. Sit down, Walker," he told the ex-heavyweight.

Walker hesitated, glowered at the Hangman, then sat.

A thin smile slashed White's lips.

Schnell cocked his head at the three black men and crooked a grin. "Let's face it. Yours is a conquered people. All of Africa is proof of that."

"Keep talkin', krautface," Barnes said.

Hangman ran an icy stare over the six cutthroats. "Look, if any of you people have a particular problem with this mission, with going to Africa, say so now. You'll be removed. And I don't have to tell you what I mean by removed."

They all stared at the Hangman. No one spoke.

"There's a quick cure for your bullshit," Hangman added. "I hope we're understanding each other."

Yeah, they understood all right.

"Okay, I'm going to lay out all the Intelligence I have on Operation Apocalypse. First, these areas here..." Hangman said, pointing at five circled spots on the enlarged map of Zaire and the Congo, "are homes to several large Catholic missions. Three of them *were*. Past tense. Something or someone torched these missions, killed every last villager and many of the nuns and priests working the missions. A priest and several nuns from one of these missions are reported missing. A UN delegation has already gone into the Congo and Zaire to investigate. They turned up nothing."

"That's about right for the UN," Walker said.

"I'm glad to hear somebody 'sides myself say the UN ain't worth a shit," White said. Then he muttered, "Even if it's you."

Hangman let out a pent-up breath and continued. "There's been no word on the attacks from the government out of Brazzaville or Leopoldville."

"Kinshasa," Barnes corrected.

"Whatever. But if there's a renegade paramilitary operation going on in the Congo, then it wouldn't be hard to hide it. Zaire alone is more than three times as big as Texas. And tropical rain forests cover more than a third of the country."

"Any idea who's behind the attacks?" Walker wanted to know. "Sounds to me like death squads."

"Sounds even more like the great white hunter at work again," Barnes added.

Hangman drew a breath, turned, looked at his troops. "There's a possibility our targets are Nazi war criminals. Who may or may not be working in collusion with the South African government."

That, the Hangman saw, went over really well with his black soldiers. And he also got Schnell's undivided attention.

Barnes shook his head. Walker snorted, "It would figure if it was. Genocide comin' out of fuckin' South Africa."

"I'll be more than happy to go to Johannesburg and do my part," Barnes grimly told Hangman.

"Christ," White said. "Listen to big 'Roots' over there. He's goin' back to the homeland. Be sure to take some ketchup with you, Sammy," he told Barnes. "The natives'll just love to see your ass in a boiling pot."

"Yeah," Williams added. "I understand your African bloods can't stand the sight of American blacks."

"What the fuck you know about Africa, honky?" Barnes rasped. "I'll tell you what *I* know, motherfucker. Whitey's over there for one thing only. To rape Africa of all its natural resources. The black man just happens to be in the way."

"And you'd better believe it's black muscle that's bringing all that gold and diamonds up out of those mines," Jackson said. "Makin' the whites there filthy fuckin' rich."

White arched an eyebrow and threw a curiously amused look at the fisherman. "So file a grievance with the NAACP. Hell, fisherman, that's why they call it *wog* work, anyway. If you read Cap'n's Intel dossier on South Africa, you'd know there ain't a white there that does manual labor. That's for the *kaffirs*."

"That's all right, cracker," Walker shot back, showing the ex-Klansman a menacing smile. "That'll just toughen us niggers up more while Whitey's sittin' on his fat ass over there. Y'know, when the blacks finally overrun the Boers and the British. Take back the land that's rightfully theirs."

"Never happen," White dryly dismissed. "Don't forget, the Zulus have a pretty good life under the Boers. Seems any of those Bantu beauties ever start rockin' the boat, the Zulus go in there and bust a few heads."

Barnes looked pointedly at Hangman. "How do you feel about all this, man?"

"Feel about what, Barnes?"

Barnes shrugged. "About the apartheid thing in South Africa. If there's a chance we're goin' there, I'd like to know just where you stand. Meaning, are your nigger soldiers gonna get out of there if you can help it?"

Hangman felt his anger edge toward rage. He didn't want this briefing to turn into one long discussion on political views. But they were all walking right into a cauldron of hatred, murder, and sabotage just about anywhere in Africa. It was a sensitive issue, damn right. One explosive situation. And all of them would soon be sitting right on top of a human time bomb. Hangman shook off the question and dismissed the meeting. The Killsquad members seemed to pick up on his mood, and there was less grumbling than he expected. As Hangman moved to follow his troops out of the briefing room, something caught his eye. The something was what Williams had scratched on his desktop with the *shuriken*. The one-eyed pirate had written STUPID NIGGER IS A DOUBLE NEGATIVE. Yeah, the SOD man thought, it was going to be one beautiful trip with some real beautiful people.

Joy to the world.

CHAPTER THREE

Someone was always pissing on his parade, the Hangman thought. At the moment, that someone happened to be the World Strike Force, the ultrasecret branch of the CIA's Special Operations Division that financed the covert search-and-destroy missions of the Hangman and his Death Row soldiers. And Hangman could tell by the grim, tight-lipped expressions on General William Winslow III and on the Deputy Director of Central Intelligence that they had a bladderful set to fly full stream all over him. This was one parade, Hangman thought, that might not get out of the parking lot.

Winslow and the DDCI, two of the highest-ranking members of the Intelligence community, were waiting on the airstrip near the black-camouflaged, fixed-wing, propjet gunship *Spooky*. They ignored the Hangman's six soldiers as they boarded the gunship. A white skull-and-crossbones insignia was painted on the hull of the gunship beside the fuselage doorway. *Spooky*'s propellers began to spin to life with a thunderous rumble of mighty engines, exhaling dust sheets over Winslow and the DDCI.

Behind the Hangman, the sun set, a blood-red eye over the *Jornada del Muerto,* the Journey of the Dead. Hangman, an Uzi submachine gun slung around his shoulder, pulled up before the five-star Air Force general and the DDCI. The short, stocky, barrel-chested Winslow had a thinning, closely cropped head of shock-white hair. His eyes were ice-blue and held the judgmental look of a fire-and-brimstone preacher. The DDCI was tall, thin, with nondescript features. He could have looked like any one of a thousand suits out of the Hill, the Hangman thought.

"Now what?" Hangman asked, forced to nearly shout over the rumble of the propjet engines.

Winslow and the DDCI just looked at the SOD man for a long moment.

"C'mon, stop pissing around," the Hangman growled. "I know you people didn't come all the way here from D.C. just to kiss me good-bye."

"No," the DDCI finally said. "We came here to give you a warning. Your last. The President was outraged."

"What are you talking about?"

"I'm talking about your actions on the last mission. When you dropped those Russian dignitaries off on the White House lawn, bound and gagged like common criminals."

"Dignitaries? What kind of crap is that?" Hangman shook his head. "You know, sometimes I think you guys ought to go take some space up at the UN. The vodka's on the taxpayers."

Anger flared in Winslow's eyes. He shook a finger at the Hangman and seemed speechless for a moment.

"That's hardly funny," the DDCI said in a flat voice.

"You and your pirates are just about out of the

picture, mister," Winslow growled. "One more fuck-up and you're history."

"If I didn't know better, General, I would believe you're almost disappointed we've successfully finished two missions . . . and lived to tell about it."

"If this mission wasn't so urgent, mister," Winslow warned, "you'd be out on your ass, and those scum would be back in the brig where they belong. You don't seem to understand the embarrassment you caused this Administration by your dumping those Rusk—Russian VIPs off like you did. You damn near sparked an international incident with the goddamn Soviets."

"How come you people always wait till the last minute to do your bitching? You must like joyriding around the countryside on Uncle Sam."

Winslow and the DDCI stood in hard silence, appearing momentarily flustered.

"If you'll excuse me, gentlemen, I've got an 'urgent' mission waiting for me," the Hangman said, turning away from the general and the DDCI.

"We're cutting back on your pay," Winslow called out.

The Hangman stopped two steps up the gangway and turned.

"We can't justify twenty thousand dollars per scum any longer," Winslow said. "In the first place, it's too damned much money. Second, it's too easily traced. As far as the chip on your shoulder about the taxpayers and the government that supports you goes, I'm sure you'll understand."

Hangman let out a pent-up breath. A cut in pay, huh. The boys in the band were really going to love that, he thought.

"So what do I tell them?" Hangman asked and jerked his head at the flying battleship.

Old Stone Face didn't change expression as he told the SOD man, "Cut in half. Ten thousand per scum. And it may go down again. Quite frankly, I hope there's not a lot of crying about this. It's not like you sonsofbitches have to answer to the IRS."

"I'll be sure to remember you guys some Christmas," the Hangman said. "Yours will be the stocking full of Charmin."

Mac White was waiting inside the doorway as the Hangman climbed into the fuselage. "What was that all about?" the ex-Klansman wanted to know.

"You'll find out soon enough."

The Hangman shut the door behind him. He pushed the intercom button on the wall and told the pilot, "Let's roll." A moment later, he felt the giant fighting bird begin to roll down the runway. The floorboard trembling beneath his boots, the sound of rolling thunder in his ears, the Hangman walked down the fuselage. His troops had taken a seat on the bench in the aft section of the cargo hold. Mac White followed at the Hangman's heels.

Spooky, the AC-47 gunship, the SOD man knew, had been quite a fearsome death machine during the Vietnam War. This particular version, on loan to the CIA and modified by the Army for the Company's antiterrorist war, sported two GE MXU-470 7.62mm miniguns, four .50-caliber machine guns mounted on the nose, two 20mm GE M61 Gatling cannons, and two 40mm Bofors cannons in the aft. The "war room" housed the Korad laser range-finder/designator, the GE ASQ-145 Low Light Level Television, and the Xerox Night Observation Device, sophisticated homing and tracking devices that could pick out enemy locations by engine and exhaust heat. In addition, *Spooky* was equipped with a Quick Fix jamming system. A flying battle-ship, damn right, the Hangman knew. Any bullshit encounters over international waters or in enemy airspace with the Soviets, Libyans, or any other hostiles, and the pilot and copilot were under orders to fight to the death. No, the Hangman thought, he wouldn't mind one bit looking out a porthole and seeing a few MIGs plunging for the ocean if *Spooky* caught them with a surprise opening burst. Hell, he'd even let Mac White open the hatch door and piss down on the flaming wreckage. And he might even let the boys in the band shoot off a few fireworks, in the event *Spooky* downed a MIG or two.

Hangman had plans for *Spooky*, hell yes.

In between missions he outlined new operations. By now he knew the WSF would be chewing over Project MeccaDung. In it, he proposed to use *Spooky* to attack suspected terrorist bases in the Middle East. *Spooky* could be modified to house eight-inch and 155mm Howitzer nuclear projectiles and 155mm Binary chemical projectiles to be used against major terrorist installations in remote regions. One complete search-and-destroy swoop over all known Arab terrorist installations that were sending out death squads into the world. Maybe even a run at Qadaffi's hardsite in Libya. *Spooky* would provide the heavy air-firepower support while he and his troops mopped up from the ground. On to Iran, then Iraq. Take care of the Persian Gulf war for both sides. Hell, after pulling it off, he thought about flying over Jerusalem on the way back to the States, maybe chute down a crate of liquor and about five hundred pounds of pork chops. On the crate, just for the hell of it, he'd write JESUS, SON OF GOD, LIVES. AND HE'S COMING BACK FOR YOU, PEOPLE. YOU CHOSEN ONES BETTER SEE IF YOU'RE HOLDING THE WRONG EDGE OF THE JUDAS BLADE. LOVE, PONTIUS.

As *Spooky* lifted off, the Hangman took a seat opposite his troops. They had all been given shots for yellow fever, smallpox, yaws, and trypanoso-miasis—sleeping sickness. Hair had been shaved off the sides of their heads, cut to a quarter-inch on the crown. Weapons issued to each soldier: a brand new Uzi submachine gun, straight out of the *Fabrique Nationale* in Belgium, and ten spare thirty-two-round clips; three MK2 frag grenades, three M15 grenades filled with twenty ounces of white phosphorus; Detonics .45 Combat Master Mark VI in handgun and four spare clips; Fairbairn-Sykes commando dagger; garotte. As on the two previous missions, Schnell and Walker were the firepower exceptions. The German mercenary and the ex-heavyweight would also carry flesh-shredding autoshotguns for in-close slaughter. The nine-shot Franchi Special Purpose Automatic Shotgun in twelve-gauge for Schnell. The twenty-round, twelve-bore Atchisson autoshotgun for Walker. After the mission supply drop, Hangman would issue the rocket firepower to Walker and White — the MM-1 Multiround Projectile Launcher. Heavy firepower all the way, Hangman knew. Another take-no-prisoners operation, damned straight.

Hangman inspected his troops. Like him, they were dressed in dark green jungle camos, reversible to black for combat night-fighting. Wide-brimmed dark green commando hats with chin straps hung from the pegs above the heads of the soldiers. At the moment, Williams had decided to wear his commando hat. On the hat, the one-eyed pirate had taped a white piece of paper that read HOORAY FOR KING LEOPOLD. LONG LIVE BELGIUM. The Hangman flashed Williams a hard-eyed look. That's one guy, the SOD man thought, who's sure going to pave the way to better international relations. *Fucking smartass.*

Hangman bent and flipped open the lid of a small box beside him. With his foot, he pushed the box across the floor.

"Pick your smokes," the SOD man said. Then cracked, "Sorry, but we're out of Virginia Slims."

White and Williams were the first ones to reach into the box full of cigarette packs and lighters. The ex-Klansman grinned, pulled out a pack of Camel unfiltereds and a Zippo lighter, and said, "Sometimes you do all right by me, Cap'n."

"I quit smoking, man." Walker rumbled.

"You'd better take it up again," Hangman said. "You'll need to keep one going while we're in the jungle."

"Why's that?" Walker wanted to know.

"Mosquitos, right, Sarge?" Williams said.

"That, and to burn the leeches off."

Hand wrapped around a pack of Marlboros, Williams froze and looked at the Hangman. The revelation, the SOD man could see, didn't go over well with any of them.

"Is that the reason for the skinhead 'do?" Williams asked. "I'm gonna have some leech suckin' the blood out of my head?"

"We'll probably have to strip down every five klicks or so," the Hangman said. "They'll lock on anywhere they can. Not just your face and head. Assholes included."

White muttered a curse. "You never make things easy for us, do ya, Cap'n?"

Hangman unfolded a map. Squatting, he spread the map over the floor. "You want it easy, White, I can arrange that right now. And I suggest you talk to your buddy Williams. King Leopold didn't exactly have a running love affair going with the Congolese."

"You got that right, Big Brother," Barnes added, throwing Williams a baleful look. "One-Eye's billboard may go over with the South Africans, but he just might find an *assegai* up his ass if he ain't careful. If he'd read your Intel, One-Eye would know that the Congo was fewer seven million Congolese at the turn of the century, thanks to the Belgians. African workers who didn't fill their work quotas were either killed by Leopold's motherfuckers or had their hands and feet cut off. For someone who never even went to Africa, Leopold got filthy fuckin' rich on rubber and ivory. Your so-called white Christian missionaries were famous for cutting off hands and feet, too, just a couple of hundred years back. Your white boys here, Big Brother, seem to think the African nigger invented savagery."

"Fuck you guys," Williams growled. "If the natives can't take a joke, fuck 'em."

"All right, shut up and listen," Hangman said. "Let me finish the brief, then you people can talk history all you want.

"Now, we'll be dropping here," he said, pointing to a red circle on the map around an enlarged area of western Zaire, "on the edge of this savanna. From there, we walk approximately twenty-five kilometers through this jungle to the mission along the Congo River."

"Why walk?" Schnell asked.

Hangman glanced at Schnell. The German had his arms folded over his chest, and there was the same funny look in Schnell's eyes that the Hangman had seen during their first mission together when the German had decided to abandon the group in search of his own freedom.

"The misions that have been attacked are due north of our assigned mission. According to Intelligence, these hits have moved in a pattern from north to south. If the village and its perimeter are being reconned for a hit, I don't want to scare off or alert our targets by our arrival. We're expected at the village by a Father Enrico Martinelli."

"An Italian padre, huh," White grumbled. "Christ."

"Maybe he'll have some red wine and spaghetti waitin' for us," Williams said.

Hangman ignored the remarks. "We'll stay with the missionaries and the native bushmen as long as it takes for us to identify the targets. Then, it's search and destroy.

"Spectre, our helicopter gunship, will be waiting along the Congo–Zaire border. Scheduled checkpoints. Aerial recon. Any air-fire support we might need. We'll make the switch to Spectre before the drop. Now in the event that the trail out of Zaire leads us to South Africa, Spectre will transport us to the Botswana–Transvaal border. You three," Hangman said, looking at his black soldiers, "will be left behind at a mission fuel depot here." He indicated an area marked off near Victoria Falls. "If we have to go into South Africa, it will be a hard hit. We'll be met by a Company contact who has already arranged for us to be inside of South Africa as part of a UN delegation speaking out against apartheid."

Walker snorted. "Give my regards to Bishop Tutu, cracker," he said to White.

Barnes chuckled. "Maybe you can wear a new billboard through the homelands, One-Eye. 'Hooray for the Voortrekkers. Long live the Boers.'"

Jackson grinned. "Yeah, man, 'I left my heart at Blood River.'"

"Okay," Hangman quietly growled, "now that everyone's in the spirit of things here, I'll continue. Item: I suggest that you keep your eyes peeled when we move through the jungle. Some of the world's deadliest snakes inhabit this region. There is no snakebite kit for the black or the green mamba. Both of which can move along the ground as fast as a man can run. And they're the only snakes known that will go out of their way to attack. Once bitten, you'll be dead inside of ten minutes. Also, watch out for the ringhals, or the spitting asp. Less than an ounce of ringhal venom in the eye, and you could be blinded permanently."

"Jesus," White said in a sour voice. "This operation's sounding better by the minute. I'll never get to Iran at this rate. And all those fuckin' *mullahs* pissin' on the American flag, just waitin' to have their Iranian asses kicked."

Hangman opened the weapons crate. From it he pulled a large, sheathed knife. He tossed the sheath to Walker. The ex-heavyweight caught the weapon and scabbard and slid the curved knife from its sheath.

"A Kukri," Schnell commented.

"Exactly," the Hangman affirmed as Walker examined the giant ceremonial knife with its razor-sharp twenty-two-and-a-half-inch blade. "We'll use them to hack our trail through the jungle. Among other things, if we have to. Another item," the Hangman said, pulling a gas mask from the crate and flipping it to Williams. "My hunch is that our targets are planning mass genocide of Central and maybe parts of South Africa. Nerve gas has been finding its way into South Africa via a black-market pipeline out of the States. The mask is just in case. Put them in your rucksacks."

"You said something about war criminals."

Hangman looked at Schnell. "There's no proof, Schnell, that your father and uncle are the targets."

"Hey, hold on a minute," Barnes said, glancing from Schnell to the Hangman. "You sayin' the German's got family who were Nazis?"

"The Surgeons, they were called," Hangman answered. "Death doctors at Auschwitz. Disappeared right after the Allies gave Russia their chunk of Germany. It's suspected by West Germany's Center for Nazi War Criminals that the Surgeons are alive and well. Current whereabouts unknown."

"I got this guy here whistling the German National Anthem," White growled, "and you expect us to trust him when our backs are turned if his old man's settin' up a Fourth Reich kill-shop in the fuckin' Congo?"

"I regret what they did." Schnell's voice was cold as ice. "If it is true, they will answer to me. I am against what they stood for. For the thousands they murdered. That is all I need to say about this matter."

"That's easy for you to say now, German," Jackson said. "But we haven't forgotten how you lit out on us during the first mission."

"Yeah," Williams added. "How the hell we know

he won't do it again? Or even decide to turn the guns on us this time?"

"Only Schnell can answer that," Hangman told Williams. "And I'm sure he will. Soon enough."

"You wouldn't care to answer that now, would you, German?" Walker said. "I mean, if it's your blood or save the niggers, what's it gonna be?"

All eyes turned to Schnell. The German soldier of fortune sat stone still, his arms folded over his chest, stare locked on the Hangman. Finally, he shrugged.

"I will answer it like this," Schnell said, grim. "Any country that can come out of nowhere twice, take on the entire world, and twice nearly win deserves to be admired. Regardless of wartime atrocities. As I recall, you *Amerikaners* had your asses handed to you for the first four years of World War Two by the German soldier. Europe was a continent crushed and conquered by my people. My country lost only because we ran out of fuel and because a madman had us fight on the West, the Russian and Africa theatres at the same time, instead of conquering one front at a time and moving on."

"What'd I tell ya, Cap'n?" White growled. "Might as well start singin' *Duetschland über Alles.*"

"Aber but," Schnell coldly said. "I will kill anyone who tries to kill me on this mission. Black or white."

"How 'bout your Aryan comrades from the Fatherland?" Williams gruffed.

"The Aryans were Indoeuropeans," Schnell corrected in an icy voice. "Closely related to the Persians in language, religion, and customs. They settled India from two thousand to six hundred B.C. They mixed with the dark-skinned Dravidians in the Indus Valley and formed the Hindu culture. It was something Hitler was dead wrong about. Persians are hardly of pure Teutonic stock."

"I hear ya, German," White allowed. "It would

piss me off to have somebody mistake me for a dungeating Iranian, too."

"Man for man," Schnell quickly said, still looking at the specialist, "there was and is no better soldier than the German soldier. Ruthless. Fearless. Dedicated. Disciplined. Superior intelligence and motivation. Whether they care to admit to it or not, many of today's military machines are modeled after Germany's Third Reich war machine, Gestapo and *Luftwaffe*. The Israelis, who have the most superior air defense and offensive in the world, learned their lesson well from the Holocaust. And the Soviets, from SPETSNAZ to the KGB to the common peasant Russian foot soldier, have mimicked Nazi Germany down to their version of the goose step. Who do you think put Lenin into power during the Bolshevik Revolution? Certainly, no Russian is original enough to come up with a system of thought the likes of Karl Marx or Friedrich Engels."

"I'll give you this much, Schnell," Hangman said. "They had the most corrupt, evil, inhuman regime in the history of the world. But the world has never seen and will never see again a war machine as formidable as Nazi Germany."

A thin smile twisted Schnell's lips. "You do not have to flatter me."

"How do you like this guy?" White growled, looked at the Hangman. "You tell him how great his people are, and he tells you to stuff it."

"I don't give a shit what any of you dudes think," Barnes said. "Apartheid. White colonial rule. Whatever. If I can help it, I sure as hell won't let happen to the blacks in Africa what happened to the Jews in Europe. I don't give a damn if it's Nazis, Boers, British, or Zulus."

A heavy silence followed the black street assassin's threatening words.

Hangman sensed the tension mounting to the breaking point of violence. He drew a breath, looked at the faces of his cutthroat lot. Regardless of how they felt about one another, he knew that when the time came, no matter who the enemy was, they would fight to the death, down to the last man. All of them, he knew, had a brutal animal instinct for self-preservation.

Mac White cleared his throat. For a moment he rubbed his hands, seemed embarrassed. "Listen, there's somethin' the German said, and that guy, too," he growled, throwing a look at Barnes, "that I gotta go along with. I know I spout off about blacks and Jews and Iranians, and I probably sound like a real redneck asshole sometimes—"

"Sometimes?" Walker rumbled.

Williams chuckled, and several of the other soldiers joined the laughter.

White frowned but pushed on. "When the bullets start flyin' at me, you'd better believe I'll be right there with you dudes."

"Yeah," Leroy Walker said, a strange smile crooking his lips. "Till death do us part."

"It's nothin' personal," White soberly said. "Hell ...I don't like anybody."

The Death Row soldiers settled into their private thoughts. Mac White appeared uncomfortable for a moment, as if he'd just laid part of his soul out on the chopping block. The ex-Klansman looked at the specialist and said, "Are we there yet, Cap'n?"

"Get some shut-eye, White," the Hangman said. "And some shut-mouth. It's going to be a long ride."

"I hear ya, Captain Honky," Walter mumbled, closing his eyes.

A long ride, yeah, the Hangman thought. Perhaps a death-ride for them all.

Straight into Hell.

Watch out, Africa. The damned, the Hangman knew, had screamed free from the left hand of Satan once more.

Tear down the voice of reason.

Let the arrows fly.

Draw the battle lines.

Let the black siren wail on.

The war machine, the Hangman knew, was ready to surge ahead.

Set on autodestruct.

Coming to rip the dark heart out of the heart of darkness.

Yeah, Hangman knew, a black sun was about to set over Africa.

CHAPTER FOUR

Pink streaks of light knifed the gray cloud cover over the jungle of Zaire. *Whump-whump-whump* sounded to the east of the tropical rain forest. Moments later, the behemoth black helicopter battleship with the skull and crossbones on its nose parted the gloomy Congo ceiling, shattering the silence over the savanna.

The Hangman stood in the open fuselage doorway, his chute pack strapped on. Six hundred feet below him, he watched the grasslands blur past Spectre. A herd of zebras scattered beneath the monstrous black warbird. Antelope and giraffes roamed the open land far to the southeast, near the edge of the plateau that bordered the savanna. There, a chain of jagged black rocks jutted up against the horizon.

Zaire, the Hangman thought. Known as the Belgian Congo from 1885 until its independence from Belgium almost three decades ago. Whatever the land was called—a land eighty times the size of its former occupier—it would always stay wild, primitive, and mysterious. Deadly, too. The white man's grave, hell yes. This was a land that geologists and anthropologists claimed had changed very little since the dawn of prehistory. An untamed land that had been first settled by Pygmies when woolly mammoths and saber-toothed tigers still walked the earth. And yeah, Hangman knew Africa had given birth to the world's oldest settled culture: Pharaonic Egypt. Africa the Ancient, now encroached upon by twentieth-century so-called civilization.

History, Hangman knew, had begun to record well-developed civilizations in southeastern Zaire only as recently as the A.D. 700s. The Kongo, Kuba, Luba, and Lunda kingdoms grew and inhabited this region in relative peace. Until the coming of Portuguese seamen in 1482 at the mouth of the Congo River. The first European explorers discovered an Iron Age civilization in the lower Congo region, a society that closely resembled the feudal system of medieval Europe. From the early 1500s to the middle 1800s, the Portuguese and other Europeans dealt in "black ivory." Tribal Kongo chieftains found it very profitable to sell their own people into slavery to the white men and the Arabs. The history of the slave trade, the Hangman knew, was quite contrary to a lot of bullshit that had flown around in his country about how white sea captains went into the bush and captured blacks for slavery.

The bullshit had also flown through Belgium when King Leopold II had received personal title to the Congo at the Berlin Conference in 1885, and the thieving, butchering sonofabitch had dared call it the Congo Free State. Barnes had been dead-on in his assessment of many of the Belgians as butchers of the Congolese. Rape of African natural resources was indeed the primary interest of most Europeans and many American businessmen. Not to mention the fucking hammer-and-sickle wielders in the

Kremlin. Hell, first of all, it was hardly racist to say that the black African was just down out of the trees. Unless, of course, it came from the emotional mouth of a Mac White, who spoke primarily out of fear and hatred. By ignoring certain facts about black Africa, the bleeding hearts and the UN had set the entire continent back a good ten centuries, dropped black Africa right into a nest of vipers. The Soviets. Yeah, by granting African countries independence too quickly and without the proper education that would ensure their own ability for self-government, the bleeding-heart shitsuckers of the free world had given black Africa plenty of rope with which to hang itself. And more of that rope was being handed over daily to the Soviets.

Sure, the native Africans had proven themselves helpless against the European colonizers.

But they were proving themselves even more helpless against the deceit and ruthlessness of the Soviet military murder machine.

Hell, just what was the answer, he asked himself. One guy had the answers. But he'd been killed by his own people. Staked to a tree about two thousand years ago.

"Hey, Sarge. Where the hell's your head?"

Hangman turned, looked at Tommy "King Leopold II" Williams. The one-eyed pirate waited, fifth in line, ahead of only Jackson. All of the Death Row soldiers were hooked up to the overhead cable.

"We just got the green light there, Cap'n," White called out.

Hangman glanced at the green light, heard the pilot's voice over the intercom as he informed, "Thirty seconds to the drop site."

The lush green foliage of the jungle loomed, three hundred meters and closing fast.

The SOD man shoved the small weapons crate out of the gunship. "Let's hit it," he ordered, nearly shouting over the deafening rotor wash. "Try not to land on any pythons or lions."

"Fifty thousand comedians out of work," Williams grumbled to Walker, "and we get stuck with the Lenny Bruce of the CIA."

"Maybe he'll get his own nightclub act when he retires, think?" White said.

The Hangman heard the remarks. Prejump jitters at work, he knew. "I already had one," he told his troops. "Hell, they're still talking about me in Poughkeepsie."

"Poughkeepsie, yeah, it figures," White said. "You ain't got enough class to go Broadway."

"Go!"

Schnell led the way out of the door, the others following. Jackson hesitated.

"Jump, damnit!" the Hangman shouted. "You wanna land in the trees?"

Jackson jumped. Hangman followed the fisherman out the door. Christ, he thought, there was nothing in the world like a good free-fall. Bless those fucking Chinese acrobats who first used parachutelike rigs in 1306. Bless Leonardo Da Vinci for drawing a sketch and keeping notes on that rigid pyramid-shaped parachute around the 1500s. Bless J. B. Blanchard who recorded the first successful use of the chute, dropping his dog in 1785, then descending safely himself in 1793. But it was the crude canvas devices used to descend from hot-air balloons in the late eighteenth and early nineteenth centuries from which the modern parachute evolved. Bless those bastards, he thought, drinks on him. Hell, the only time he felt free was when he was falling back to earth. Of course, the combat jumps were short-lived, and he'd rather go with a HALO jump anyday. Strap on the bail-out bottle and leap out at the earth from thirty thousand feet up. Excessive parachute opening shock, the hell with it. Frostbite or no frostbite, fuck it. *Hello, HALO.*

Before he knew it, this combat jump was over. He hit the tall grass on the balls of his feet and rolled.

"Jesus Christ. Jesus Christ!"

Shucking out of his pack, Hangman leapt to his feet. Uzi in hand, he looked toward the jungle from where the voice of panic and terror came, searching for that guy who was boisterously breaking one of the Ten Commandments.

Williams was hung up in the trees, dangling from his harness. Desperately, the one-eyed pirate clawed for his commando dagger. A second later, the Hangman saw the reason for the pirate's frenzy.

Williams had landed in a nest of mambas. Long, slender green and black serpents slithered down the canopy and twisted down the rizors. Barnes, Schnell, and White were closest to the jungle. They reacted instantly to the threat of death that was gliding down the chute for Williams.

Hangman joined the blistering roar of weapons fire. A hurricane of 9mm flesh-shredders blazed up at the tree line. Schnell's SPAS-12 bucked, thundered repeatedly. While Williams sliced at his straps, bits and pieces of black and green snakeflesh rained over him. A Parabellum slug exploded the head of a mamba as it lunged for Williams's neck. The Death Row soldiers sprayed the nest until the one-eyed pirate cut himself free and dropped to the ground.

Terror had gripped Williams. Whirling, the one-eyed pirate cut loose with his Uzi, raking the tree line with a long barking burst until the clip went dry. The thick, green broccoli-shaped foliage seemed to writhe as the mamba nest scattered.

The air rasping past Williams's lips was the only sound for long moments.

Barnes chuckled. "Hey, man."

Williams turned and looked at the black street assassin.

"You want your hat back, don't ya?"

Williams followed Barnes's laughing stare. He found his commando hat snagged in the vines near the top of the tree line. A slender, glistening thread coiled around the crown with the one-eyed pirate's personal message from Belgium.

"Long live King Leopold," Barnes laughed, grim-faced.

Hangman broke open the weapons crate. Quickly, he handed out the MM-1s to Walker and White.

The ex-Klansman looked at the squat, revolver-shaped rocket launcher and smiled. "Was hopin' you'd bring this baby along, Cap'n."

"Think you can handle that thing?" Walker rumbled.

"Hell you talkin' about now?" White growled.

"Let's stop the jawing, all right. We've got a long hike," Hangman told his troops, then moved down along the outer fringes of the jungle, searching for any sign of a possible trail. After a thirty-minute search, he found the closest thing to a path into the gloomy nest of trees and mangrove.

The soldiers gathered around the SOD man. None of them appeared eager to venture into the dark bowels of Zaire.

"Who's walking point?" Mac White asked.

"You are," the Hangman answered.

White cursed, shook his head. "Figures," he said, then hesitated, peering into the tangled wall of vines and overhanging plants. "Maybe we oughta wait until there's a little more sunlight, huh, Cap'n?"

"It won't get any lighter in there, White. What the hell do you want? Some flashing strobe lights? This isn't a disco. Get the lead out."

Cursing, the ex-Klansman unsheathed his Kukri. One angry swipe of the fearsome blade cut away an overhang of thorny vines. Howls, screams, a buzzing din of insect chatter swept over the Hangman and his Death Row soldiers as they moved into the jungle.

"Which way, Cap'n?"

"Just keep walking," the Hangman said, pulling out his magnetic compass. "We want north by northwest. I'll handle all the azimuth and back-azimuth action from back here."

"Yeah, I hear ya'," the ex-Klansman grumbled, swiping at the brush.

"Just keep your toes and fingers handy, cracker," Walker chuckled. "In case we need somebody to count."

"Fuck you."

"Shut up, all of you," Hangman wearily growled.

Immediately, the SOD man felt the leeches as they landed on his arms and neck, falling from the jungle canopy or attaching themselves as he brushed against a tree. Trees so fat that two men could put their arms around them without touching hands. With their Zippos, everyone fired up a cigarette.

Jackson sucked greedily from one of his three canteens.

Williams started pulling the leeches off his arms.

"Leave 'em alone," Hangman called out. "You pull them off, you'll rip off the pincers which will stay in your skin. The last thing you want out here is an infection."

"Ya' little fuckers," Williams snarled, mashing a leech over his arm with the palm of his hand, blood bursting from the inch-and-a-half sucker like a squashed water balloon.

Kukris swished back and forth, clearing away patches of vines and brush that blocked the narrow path. Shadows danced over the CIA kill-team, where shafts of light knifed through the foliage. In most places, though, visibility was only a few yards. The going was slow and difficult. Eventually, Hangman worked his troop in shifts for the point detail. Boots squished over the spongy ground wet with ancient leafmold. The deeper they penetrated into the jungle, the darker it seemed to get. Within two hours, the heat and humidity grew so oppressive, it felt to the Hangman as if they were walking through a sauna. His clothes were drenched in sweat. His face and arms were cut, streaked with blood, and masked with leeches. Clouds of mosquitos swarmed over the Killsquad column every step of the way. The dense jungle canopy seemed to howl, screeching with bird and animal life. The powerful stench of a millenium of decay hung in the air like the rot of flesh in an airtight tomb.

Peering in all directions, searching the black jungle recesses, the Hangman detected shadows. All around them. A warning bell sounded in his head. There was an itch on his back, right between his shoulder blades. Something stalked them.

"Hey, Cap'n," White suddenly called out. "We're coming up to something."

Ahead, Hangman saw the sunlight-drenched grass plain. It was a small area of bushland, beyond which stretched more jungle. It would do, though, for a short breather.

"Stop on the other side. Strip down and get the leeches off."

At the far edge of the clearing, the Death Row soldiers began to strip while the Hangman stood guard. He scoured the gloomy patch of jungle behind him. Damn, he thought, what was it? What the hell was out there? Was he just getting edgy? Hell no, he decided. Something in numbers was following them. He'd swear to it.

The soldiers were eager to burn the leeches off. But, as he'd suspected, the Hangman heard the usual grumbling and remarks.

"Bend over and check each other's assholes, too," he ordered.

White froze as he lowered his pants. "What the hell?" He looked at Walker, then back at the Hangman. "C'mon, you ain't serious? I gotta be lookin' up this guy's ass?"

"Just shut up and do it," Hangman growled, his attention turned to the other side of the clearing. "You've got five minutes, then we're heading on."

"Jesus! What the—God damn! Goddamn!"

All eyes turned to Mac White as the ex-Klansman dropped his pants.

"Shit!" White howled. "I got one on my dick! I got one on my dick!"

The other soldiers quickly checked themselves.

Walker chuckled, relieved. "Don't worry, cracker. He ain't gonna hurt nothin',"

Williams joined the laughter. "Hell, that little sucker's having a tough time fittin' on that thing."

"Shut your face, One-Eye," White rasped, burning the leech off his cock with the tip of his cigarette. "I'm lookin' at you, and I don't see no horsecock, either."

A wry grin started to twist the Hangman's lips as he looked away from his troops.

Then he saw the arrows streak forth from the jungle across the clearing. With lightning speed, he hit the ground a millisecond before the arrow tip thunked into the tree behind him.

Hangman opened up with his Uzi.

The soldiers froze for a second. Then the arrows started drilling into the ground in front of them. Curses, shouts of anger and panic ripped the air.

The Pygmies had caught them all off guard.

Caught them with their pants down.

Mac White tripped as he scrambled to pull his pants up.

Arrows blurred, whistling across the clearing.

CHAPTER FIVE

It wasn't exactly a reenactment of the Battle of Blood River or the Battle of Ulundi, Hangman thought. But then again, Pygmy bushmen weren't exactly in the same league as the Zulu *impis*. And with a cyclic rate of six hundred fifty 9mm Parabellum slugs per minute, the Hangman and his Death Row soldiers had the decided edge in firepower over bows and arrows, for damn sure. The quick one-sided fight, the SOD man thought, would have brought a tear of regret to the eye of the military genius and megalomaniacal Zulu chieftain, Chaka. And maybe if Cetshwayo had owned a few Uzis — or at the very least, a few hundred muskets — instead of the *assegai*, the Zulus could have run the Brits and Boers out of Africa. Yeah, the Zulus, the Southern Hemisphere's most fierce war machine in the second and third decades of the nineteenth century, could have piled a few Anglo bones in "laager" boats at the Cape of Good Hope before the Brits and

Boers cast off for Europe. *So long, white man. So good of you to visit. But you'd better get back to the queen bee, honky cat. Trade you a hundred Hottentots, though, for a white woman.*

Christ, he thought, if he could step back in time, he would've made a fortune on the international arms market. He wasn't sure, though, who he would've allowed to conquer the world. Germans, probably. Italians, maybe. But only if their women would shave under their arms and he could train a few Italians in electrolysis. There was something about a woman with a mustache. And the French? No way. Any country that could come up with a Marquis de Sade would most likely have some peculiar ideas about the disposal of human sewage. The Greeks? Hell, they hadn't been worth a shit since Roman mongrelization and Persian invasion. Since the kingdoms of the Diadochi, following Alexander the Great's death, had degenerated into guile, treachery, bribery, and the complete use of mercenary armies. *Ah, yes, the great democracy of ancient Greece.*

Hangman's initial *Uziel Gal* burst repulsed the Pygmy attack, drove them back into the jungle. His troop, though, naked as the day they came kicking out of Momma's womb and looking to kick the shit out of the world, fired a long fusillade. Pants half pulled up, blood streaking their torsos where leeches had been crushed when they'd hit the ground, Uzis blazed in the hands of five Death Row soldiers. Tommy Williams, the last one to reach cover, howled in pain, but the one-eyed pirate's sudden cry was drowned by the roar of SMG fire.

"Hold your fire!" Hangman yelled, crouched behind a tree. "Hold your fire!"

"Hold your goddamn fire!" Mac White bellowed.

Jackson kept triggering his Uzi until White banged him on the shoulder.

A deafening silence followed. The Hangman and

his troops searched the jungle across the clearing. There, shredded leaves fluttered to the ground.

"Think I saw a UN delegation over there, Cap'n," White tautly cracked, grim-faced. "Spearheaded by Teddy Kennedy and Amy Carter. They were crying, *'Free the Pygmies from white oppression.'*"

What the fuck? Hangman thought, fighting down the laughter that threatened to break through the ice ball of tension in his gut. *That was one guy they would close the Gates on in a hurry after he checked out. At least Mac White and King Leopold would have something to talk about while they were splashing around in the River Styx.*

"Damn. Goddamn," Jackson breathed, shaking his head. "Every time the fucking unexpected starts like this, it only gets worse. Shit!"

"As much as I hate to admit it, you may be right this time, fisherman," White said. "'Specially since we're out here in the middle of voodooland."

"Hey, Sarge."

All eyes turned toward Williams. Grimacing, the one-eyed pirate limped toward the group. With one hand he held his pants up around his waist. The other hand was clenched around the arrow embedded in his ass-cheek.

Barnes chuckled.

"These things poisonous?" Williams wanted to know, teeth gritted.

"If it was, you'd be dead by now," Hangman answered.

Grunting, the one-eyed pirate slid the arrow free from his ass. Blood ran from the wound and streamed down his leg. "I can clean it up, but I'll need somebody to bandage it."

The others looked pointedly at the Hangman. White laughed. "Sounds like a job for you, Cap'n."

Hangman's lips twisted slightly. "Yeah, I know," he quietly growled, standing. "I've gotten pretty good at handling asses."

* * *

The Hangman couldn't recall seeing a cloud in the sky back at the clearing. That changed, though, within the hour. Now a torrential rainfall crashed through the jungle canopy. Mercilessly, the water pelted the Killsquad column as they hacked their way down the trail. And the rain did nothing to cool any of them off. The moisture, trapped beneath the canopy, created a sticky, stinking steam. The Hangman's soldiers were angry and miserable. And they let him know it. He heard their curses clearly through the pounding waterfall. They cursed him, each other, the jungle. And he was just about at the end of his rope, too. The leeches now attached themselves to his body by the dozens, like magnets. Bleeding cuts riddled his body. His boots were not only filled with water, but, worse, he knew his socks were soaked with blood from busted leeches. With the thorny brush tearing their shirts and pants, it wasn't hard to understand how a bloodsucker could attach itself to a man's cock or testicles.

Finally, the rain stopped. But the heat intensified. The arduous march was now like wading through a boiling cauldron.

"How's that big back-azimuth action goin' there, Stanley?" Mac White called out.

Hangman looked at his compass, then met White's questioning gaze. A Pygmy's arrow had found its way through the crown of the ex-Klansman's commando hat. For reasons unknown to any of the others, White had left the arrow stuck through the crown

"I'd say we're anywhere from thirty to forty degrees off course," Hangman said.

"What?" White barked.

"In other words," Hangman said, "we're lost."

"Hey, you wouldn't bullshit us about that, would ya, Cap'n?" White said.

Limping, Williams—next to last in the column

in front of the SOD man—rubbed his wounded cheek. "Maybe we oughta hire some fuckin' Pygmy scouts to get us there."

Suddenly, a horrible screeching ripped the air. White yelled and froze. Directly above the ex-Klansman, a baboon jumped up and down on a thick branch. The baboon hissed, spat down at White.

"You stupid sonofabitch!" White rapsed, starting to raise his Uzi, then stopped and hurriedly went back to hacking his way up the trail. The ex-Klansman swiped at the baboon spittle on his face, muttering, "You dirty little cocksucker."

Barnes laughed. "Hey, cracker, c'mon. That was King Leopold the Second. Reincarnated."

Jackson and Walker laughed, too.

"What the hell is with you and that guy, huh?" White growled back at Barnes. "Guy's been dead for a hundred fucking years. Give the sonofabitch a break, will ya?"

Flicking his Zippo, Schnell fired up a Camel. He was sick and tired of listening to their ignorant tripe. *Nein*, he corrected himself, he had an acid bellyful of two missions with the *Amerikaners*. *Scheisskopfs*. All of them. Since the drop at the savanna, he had considered putting all of them out of their misery. The green-eyed CIA bastard, too. One quick Uzi burst. *Nein*. If he decided to waste them, he knew he would use the SPAS. He wanted to see their bones explode into countless fragments. He wanted to see the blood vomit from their wounds and spray like snot in a sneeze. He wanted to piss and shit on their dead bodies. He wanted to feed their guts to the fucking baboons. *Ja*, he had been so fucking sorely tempted to unleash the autoshotgun on all of them back at the clearing. But something had held his rage in check. Fate, he feared, was about to play a cruel joke on him. Destiny, he believed, had guided him to this place in Hell, to this time when he must confront the terrible, haunting past of the Fatherland. His father! His uncle! *Here?* If it was true, if he came face-to-face with his flesh and blood, with two of the greatest butchers in the world, he wasn't sure how he would react. Perhaps, he thought, at the moment of truth he would turn the guns on the *Amerikaners*. He just didn't know. He wasn't even sure he knew himself anymore.

"Hey, German?"

Schnell turned. It was the biggest *neger*. That one, he decided, would be the first to go. Schnell grunted.

"Just checkin' to see where your head is, man," Walker rumbled. "When you get real quiet like that, I get the feeling some strange shit's goin' through your head."

Schnell looked away from Walker. He took a deep drag on his Camel. By drawing the harsh smoke into his lungs, he hoped to control the murderous fury he felt burning in his belly. It didn't work.

The Congo, he knew, was about to play someone's death knell.

They weren't exactly greeted with open arms when they reached the Catholic mission village along the Congo River. But then again, the white merc in Africa, the dogs of war, had a notorious image. To most black Africans the white merc was the Black Plague in white skin. But as long as the shithead politicians and dictators of the world jerked the strings on the puppet masses, the mercenary soldier would be used—in most cases, unfortunately, by the sonofabitch holding the most cash. But these people would never believe the seven of them weren't the everyday run-of-the-mill dogs of war. *Tell that to the fucking asshole UN,* he thought.

Williams was the last one to clear the dense brush. Hobbling, cursing, he swatted at the thick swarms of tsetse flies. Slowly, the Hangman led his troops into the village. He stopped in the middle of a ring of mud-and-branch frame huts, his troops gathering around him. They all looked as if they had just stepped out of the bowels of Hell. Blood caked their torn, slashed camos. Leeches clung to their flesh. His soldiers, he noted, held their weapons at port arms as they searched the village. The fuckers never let up, he thought.

All activity in the village had ceased. Women carrying jugs of water on their heads froze near bubbling pots. Men brandishing large knives ceased gutting fish or matting grass nets. Three large crocodiles, partially skinned and gutted, were laid out near bushels of bananas. There, brown swirling clouds hung. Even from a distance, the Hangman could hear the faint buzz of mosquito swarms. Elsewhere, goats and black dogs wandered the fringes of this large Bashongo village. The naked upper bodies of many Negro women were scarred with welts where they had cut their flesh and rubbed ashes or oil into the wounds as part of their native body adornment.

There was one Bashongo woman, though, who had not disfigured her body. She stood near a hut beside the "dogs of war." And she had captured undivided attention from Barnes and Walker.

"Get your minds back to business," Hangman told the two black soldiers. "I didn't bring you halfway around the goddamn world to make a love connection."

A small naked boy ran into a large hut at the north end of the village. Moments later, a short, dark-haired man in a white robe stepped out of the hut. The specialist noted the Land Rover parked beside the priest's hut.

"Must be our Italiano padre," White said.

A tall, muscular Negro with a leopard-skin cap, a medal, and a necklace of leopards' teeth hanging around his neck followed the priest out into the sun-washed village.

"These people don't exactly look thrilled to see us

here, Sarge," Williams grumbled. "You sure this is the right place? I wasn't looking for the Holiday Inn, but this is shittin' Watts in the fuckin' boonies."

The silence weighed in on the Hangman. Ignoring the remarks from his troops, he waited as the priest and the village chieftain walked up to him. The priest studied the Hangman and his soldiers with a dark, piercing stare for long moments. The Hangman read the suspicion in the deep-set, watery black pools of the Bashongo chief's eyes loud and clear, too.

"I am Father Enrico Martinelli. I must say you don't look like any UN delegation," the priest finally said.

"The man who told you we'd be coming wasn't from the UN, either, Father," Hangman said.

The priest grunted. "Mercenaries."

"Soldiers, Father," the Hangman corrected, "who've come to make sure your village stays standing."

"I see." Martinelli clasped his hands behind his back. "Soldiers, mercenaries.... In this part of the world you all stand for the same thing. Violence and blood money. The very things which are destroying Africa."

Why did he always have to listen to this kind of shit? He didn't expect the guy to come to him on bended knee, but if the priest wanted to save his ass, he'd better lighten up. The Hangman just wasn't in the mood to listen to how *evil his breed was*. How come the self-righteous never said this about the Soviets? Or the fucking Muslim fanatic terrorists?

"If you've got a peaceful solution to what's wiping out these Catholic missions, I'm ready to hear it, Father," the SOD man said. "But unless these people turn tail and head home, you're stuck with us. So let's talk, find out what the fucking hell's going on. Then we can take care of the problem and get the fuck out of your hair."

Martinelli appeared offended for a second, then smiled bitterly. *Offended—fuckin'A—yeah,* Hangman hoped. He always liked to draw the line and let some sonofabitch know where he stood.

"So you say," he sighed, then raked a hard gaze over the six soldiers around the Hangman. "Understand this first. We have been here for thirty years. My mission has cured disease. Ended starvation. Converted the Bashongos to Christianity and forced them to do away with cannibalism and human sacrifice. We have educated and helped the Bashongo and other Congo tribes to survive where the French, the Portuguese, and the Belgians neglected—and openly violated—their human rights. I will not have a band of mercenaries suddenly come along out of nowhere and undermine the work we have done here. You can stay, yes. But you will have no contact with any of the villagers. You will not leave your weapons unattended. And you will understand that you men are not our saviors. Only Christ Jesus is the true savior. Not criminals and thugs who kill for money."

Walker looked at the young girl who'd caught his eye the moment he walked into the village. His gaze wandered over her large, cone-shaped breasts and long, slender legs. He smiled at the girl, but slowly turned his attention back to Martinelli as the priest growled, "Any sign that you are here for any other purpose than to protect us from the death squads, and you will be asked to leave."

White patted his Uzi. "Tell that to my Israeli buddy here, padre, when the lead starts flying at you."

"Shut up," Hangman warned.

Martinelli clenched his jaw, opened his mouth to say something to the ex-Klansman. Then a wail ripped through the air. All eyes turned toward the lone hut at the western edge of the village. From inside that hut a voice chanted in Bantu. Skulls and human bones flanked the doorway and lined the windowsill. Dried-out hippo hide and stuffed crocodile heads hung from the walls of the hut.

"Zumba," the Bashongo chief said, his voice a deep bass rumble as he turned and rested a hard stare on the Hangman and his soldiers. "He says there is evil in the air. He says the white men and their black dogs bring death."

"Who the hell you callin' a black dog, nigger?" Barnes rasped.

"Shut the fuck up. All of you," Hangman growled. "Look, is there someplace we can talk in private, Father?"

Silently, Martinelli turned, heading toward his hut.

The Hangman followed the priest and the Bashongo chief. Killsquad hesitated and looked around the village.

"Place gives me the fuckin' creeps," White muttered, then looked at the crocodile hides. He turned to Walker and cracked, "If we're good little dogs of war, though, we might get a new pair of shoes out of this. What do you think, champ? Is this home where the heart is, or what?"

Walker looked at the ex-Klansman with menace but said nothing.

The chant grew into a shrill singsong incantation.

Williams squashed a leech against his arm. "Got ya, asshole."

CHAPTER SIX

"It pains me to admit this," Father Martinelli said as he motioned for the Hangman and his Death Row dogs of war to take a seat at the large wooden table in the center of his quarters, "but I believe force may have to be used to stop whatever horror has now befallen this country. God in Heaven... forgive me for saying that."

No, Hangman didn't find it too strange that the priest was singing a different tune suddenly. Martinelli had spoken his antiwar piece already, gotten a lot of turn-the-other-cheek bullshit out of his system. Hell, Hangman thought, the noblest of Christians often had a way of doing that when somebody was out to hang him up by the balls. Martyrdom, in the minds of just about any Christian zealot, he believed, was good only if death was quick. And painless.

Quickly, the SOD man took in the priest's Spartanly furnished quarters. A cot, medicine cabinet, iron sink basin, wooden chairs and tables crowded the room. A bookshelf stocked with literature from the works of Karl Marx to various history books about Central and South Africa stood against the far wall. A large crucifix hung over a table which supported an opened Bible and a gold chalice.

Hangman's soldiers, toting their weaponry, having burned the leeches from their bodies, each took a seat at the priest's table. As Schnell, Walker, White, and Williams flicked Zippos to fire up cigarettes, Hangman glanced at the Bashongo chieftain. Martinelli had introduced the chief as Munanga Huumanda—a big, brooding lion of an African with a fiery stare that could drop an *assegai* in midair. Yeah, that was one Bashongo buck, he decided, who looked as if he could hold his own against anything short of a bull rhino.

"Okay, Father, you need our help. I'm glad we can agree on that. What I need to know is exactly what you know. Everything. Even if you think it's unimportant. We'll take it from there."

The priest sighed, rubbed the bridge of his nose for a moment as if he were in deep anguish. "It started about a year ago. About the time the crocodiles began moving downriver. The Bashongo witch doctors said it was a sign of a great evil to come.

"First, villagers from neighboring Bakongo tribes started vanishing. Then the rumors started. Wild stories going through the villages about armed white men coming down from the skies in great birds of death and seizing villagers. These white men, it was said, flew in great birds that sprayed fire like a dragon.

"Zaire, I'm sure you know, has gone through tremendous turmoil and seen one bloodbath after another since the Belgians granted the Congolese their independence. There has been a period of 'quiet rest' the past several years; the thought of some new revolution or even an invasion from Shaba or Angola has worried the Congolese.

"At first, I thought the disappearances of the villagers was part of some Katangan invasion or, worse, a Cuban invasion from Angola. But recently I sent some of the men from this village north, up the river, to scout out an area that was supposed to be some sort of slave-labor camp."

"And?" the Hangman pushed when Martinelli paused heavily.

"The stories, it seems, are true. Armed white men oversee hundreds of Congolese. I didn't want to believe it at first, but I went and saw it for myself. The Congolese are forced to work in mines, deep in the Kolsaba region."

"Where is the Kolsaba?"

"Maybe forty miles north. There's a road, a bad one, that leads to the valley. There's a train that runs through the valley, but it doesn't appear to go south to Kinshasa. The workers have built an extension of the tracks that run southeast and northeast."

"Do you know what the workers are hauling out of those mines?"

A bitter half-smile formed on Martinelli's lips. "It's not cobalt, I assure you."

"Diamonds? Gold? What?"

"Diamonds, mostly. Zaire is the world's leading producer in industrial diamonds. But this is not a Zairian mine."

"How do you know that?"

"How many Zairians would wear a red band with a swastika? How many helicopter gunships do you know that would have the insignia of the SS *Totenkopf*? The death's-head."

Hangman felt an ice ball immediately swell in his guts.

"Then it *is* Nazis," Barnes rasped.

"How, God in Heaven, I don't know," the Catholic priest said. "But I've seen the black-and-brown uniformed white soldiers. I've seen the helicopter gunships flying over the river. Certainly, somebody in Mobutu's government must know about this."

"They do, Father, bank your sweet frankincense and myrrh on it," Hangman growled. "Some sonsof-bitches in Kinshasa are getting a nice fat cut of whatever comes out of those mines. Tell me more about this train. How often does it go through?"

"Munanga Huumanda and his men tell me every three days," the priest answered. "Tomorrow would be another third day, if the train is running on that schedule. Sometimes it runs south from the mines, sometimes north."

"Okay," the Hangman said, addressing Father Martinelli as well as his troops. "It looks like that mine's as good a place as any to start. We'll catch some rest, then head out for a recon of that mine at 0300. If we get lucky, we might take a little train ride. You three," he said, looking at his black soldiers, "will stay and mind the store. Try to keep a low profile, huh? Just in case any enemy faces show themselves." He looked at Martinelli. "I'll need to borrow that Land Rover, Father."

Martinelli nodded. "It's yours for as long as you need it."

"Christ," White said, showing Martinelli a crooked smile. "You just said the wrong thing there, Padre. You ain't never seen how Cap'n handles a set of wheels. 'Specially when those wheels ain't his."

Hangman ignored the remark. "Any bullshit starts to go down," he told his black troops, "you've got the green light to terminate all numbers with extreme prejudice. That all right with you, Father?"

Martinelli looked at the Hangman for a moment and drew a deep breath. "Do I have a choice?"

"No."

Alois Schnell took the SS cap out of his desk drawer. For a moment, he looked at the *Totenkopf* medallion just above the shiny black leather beak. *Glory,* he heard a voice from the past call to him. *Oh, glory to the Fatherland. Where have you gone?*

The death's-head. *Ja.* It had been an emblem of

terror, a symbol of German supremacy across the entire European continent. *Years...so many years ago....* The Third Reich was dead, he thought. But the Fourth Reich was about to rise. Like the phoenix from its ashes. As the Third Reich had arisen under the ruthlessly skilled guidance of the SS.

The time had come.

Alois remembered growing up in a Germany that seemed to be dying. Foreign troops were on the soil of his beloved land, and the great Teutonic people were wracked by poverty, unemployment, and inflation. But a nation's misery, he recalled, often had a way of evoking an outraged patriotism. *Der Führer* was appointed Chancellor of Germany by Hindenburg on January 30, 1933, and Schnell had been by Hitler's side since he proclaimed himself leader of the National Socialists. Hitler, he thought, had been right. The Jews were suffocating Germany with their evil manipulation of the economy and public life.

"Führer befiehl, wir folgen," Schnell murmured to himself, his mind sinking even deeper into the dark glory days.

As a black-uniformed SS *Hauptmann* under the leadership of Himmler, Schnell had taken an active and lethal hand in the *Blood Putsch* and had quickly risen in ranks, leading the Nazi warriors into Jewish ghettos, herding up the vermin of the Fatherland for the cattle cars that would take them to the concentration camps. *Ja*, he remembered. The days of German greatness. Of Teutonic glory and victory.

Where had the glory of the Fatherland gone?

He would lead the way of the Fourth Reich, he swore to himself. He would seize or he would annihilate any black African country that resisted. Genocide by nerve gas. First villages, then cities like Leopoldville and Brazzaville. Then southward. On to Rhodesia and Angola, Botswana and Mozambique. The "antiapartheid" puppet rulers he would put into power in the RSA and the SADF—after the assassinations, after the revolution—would clear the way for his seats of power in Pretoria and Cape Town. By then, his *Amerikaner* pipeline would have shipped all the uranium, plutonium, and technology needed for him to turn the RSA into a world nuclear power. As he worked on conquering the entire Dark Continent, he would have agents, saboteurs inside East Germany and other satellite countries. They would foment the unrest that was already gnawing at the bowels of those Communist-controlled colonies. They would spearhead the revolution against the Marxist bastards. They would seize military bases and nuclear missile sites. They would train the missiles on Moscow, Leningrad. They would tear down the Berlin Wall, and East and West *Furor Teutonicus* would reunite.

The true Teutonic people, the rightful inheritors of the Thousand Year Reign, the ones who still believed in the destiny of the German people, would be flown to the RSA by the Fourth Reich. Europe, Alois Schnell thought, would soon become a thermonuclear wasteland. There could be no other way. Europe would have to be used to weaken and, one hoped, dismantle the Soviet and NATO war machines. Let the vultures gather, he thought. Let the forces of Armageddon roll onto the battle plains. He would take his chances. He was an old man with very little time left.

And he had nothing to lose.

The SS man rested his cap on his head. Quickly, Schnell strode to the far corner of his quarters. There, beneath a banner of *der Führer*, lay a large black chest with a swastika banner drapped over the top. Schnell unlocked and opened the chest. For long moments, he stood staring down into the chest, eyes glittering, a wide smile slashing his lips. Beneath him was the treasure of Africa. The treasure of the gods. But only a mere handful of the treasure of the revolution. Rare jadeite. Green and blue zircon crystals glistening under the ceiling light. A winking kaleidoscope of sapphire and rubies. Creamy white pearls from the Persian Gulf and yellow pearls from Australia's Shark Bay. And the king of gems, the God of gods. Diamonds. Most of his precious stones, he knew, were over one hundred carats.

"Kamerad Reichsführer."

Startled, Schnell slammed the lid down. No eyes were allowed to see the treasures of the revolution. The heart of a thief, he knew, was blackest in a man's comrade.

Snapping his head sideways, Schnell found Henry Vaalskrang standing in the doorway. A Boer with a lineage that went back to the Great Trek of the Voortrekkers. Vaalskrang, Schnell knew, was a man who was proud of his heritage and, like his Dutch ancestors, believed apartheid was part of God's will. And Vaalskrang, formerly of the Bureau of State Security, believed fiercely in the white man's triumph over all of Africa, black and Muslim.

Despite the fact that Schnell ordered all of his South African soldiers to address him in German and don the colors of the SS, he could never hope for an unquestioning devotion to the Reich. It disturbed him. They were, after all, Dutch. Vaalskrang, he decided, would be good, but only up to a point. Outside of himself, his brother, and a handful of German dissidents and terrorists, there was very little pure Teutonic blood in this new Reich. It was something he had vowed to change from the outset.

"What?" the SS man snapped.

"There has been some trouble, sir. Our source in Johannesburg has reported the deaths of our main suppliers in the United States."

Schnell's gaze narrowed.

"They were murdered, sir. But the last shipment of uranium was reported to have reached Cape Town safely."

Murdered? There was only one logical assumption. Someone, he feared, knew about their operation in the Congo.

"Has there been a leak from inside Mobutu's regime in Leopoldville?"

The Dutchman shook his head. "No, sir. None that we know of."

It had to be one of the filthy, fucking, ignorant blacks in this new Zaire, he thought. *Stupid bastards*. It made no difference if he'd bought their silence and approval with Nazi gold. They were not to be trusted. Schnell nodded several times, his eyelids slitting over a dark, pensive stare. Folding his hands behind his back, he began to pace back and forth in front of his desk.

"We must act quickly now. I want the gunships loaded immediately. I want you to radio von Komstaag. Tell him to have his men waiting for us along the Botswana border. We deliver tomorrow. It must begin."

"As you wish, General Field Marshal."

Schnell returned the Dutchman's salute. He waited until Vaalskrang left, then swiftly moved back to his black chest. Opening the chest, Schnell's eyes widened.

The gold death's-head on his cap reflected the light glinting off the chestful of gems.

Ja, he thought. The dawn of a new sun was about to rise over Africa. The dawn of the Fourth Reich.

CHAPTER SEVEN

Hangman checked the luminous dial of his Seiko. 0245. Damn near time to head out. He was rested, cleaned up, and had a comfortable bellyful of food. One ear listening to the conversation his troops began, he fired up his last Camel unfiltered. Yeah, he thought, touching the flame from his Zippo to the smoke, that good old psychological nicotine disease was creeping up on him again. Hell, if anything could drive him to advanced stages of emphysema and a couple of month-long drunks that would make any Irishman proud, it was the six cut-throat sonsofbitches behind him. At the moment, Mac White was splashing around in a large pot, cleaning the jungle scum off his bear-sized frame. A couple of Bashongo boys, Hangman saw, were hanging around the pot, pointing, laughing at the ex-Klansman.

"Jesus Christ," White growled. "You little fuckers act like ya never seen a white man before."

Barnes laughed. "Just never seen one so ugly, that's all."

Precombat nerves, Hangman knew. All of them edgy, itching to get on with it. Hangman stared out at the black wall of jungle trees. The howls and the distant screeches of the denizens washed over the large village by the Congo River. *Nazis, huh,* he thought, drawing a deep lungful of harsh smoke. If Zaire had granted Nazi war criminals asylum— even given the bastards the thumbs-up on a slaughter operation, a massive invasion into neighboring African countries—there was no telling who or how many cocksuckers were involved in such a conspiracy. Hangman knew there was only one place to start. Drive right into the heart of the monster and rip it out.

Hangman heard Killsquad talking among themselves.

"So fucking what if South Africa and Israel are our allies."

Hangman cocked his head. Mac White was donning his torn jungle fatigues. And the ex-Klansman was also donning the voice of reason for the white supremacists.

"Both those countries are surrounded by their enemies. What the fuck's your point about that anyway, fella?" the ex-Klansman growled at Barnes.

Softly, Hangman shook his head. The conversation droned on behind him. No discussion among his cutthroats was ever friendly.

"White racism at its finest," Barnes growled.

"Talk about racism," Hangman heard White shoot back at the black street assassin. "That fuckin' desecration you wear around your neck's gonna get ya a few extra eons in Hell, fella."

"This 'desecration,' cracker, happens to be fact. Jesus Christ was dark-skinned."

"Bullshit. Hell, even if he was, he wasn't black."

Next stop, papal Rome, Hangman thought. The Vatican would never be the same.

"History has proven that black African countries cannot independently govern themselves."

Schnell. Talk about a guy with an open mind, Hangman thought.

"All right, all right," he growled, walking up to his own circle of *Agronsky and Company*. "A little rest, I can see, does you people a world of good. You three," he said to his white troop, "grab your gear. We're heading out. And you three," he said to his black troop, recalling how interested they had seemed in the village women, "keep your pants on while we're gone."

"Yeah," Mac White growled, picking up his Uzi and MM-1 rocket launcher. "I don't think Welfare'll cover you guys here."

"You're gonna get your fat white head handed to you someday, cracker," Walker threatened.

"Sure. Talk to my agent and promoter here," White said, following the Hangman toward the Land Rover. "We'll set something up. And you'd better train with more than just your mouth."

The Land Rover jounced over the narrow dirt road as if the vehicle's fat tread were setting off mines. Baobab and lacy groves of fern-covered palm trees flanked the road like sentinels. Dousing the lights after passing a trading post, the Hangman had nearly sideswiped a lion and her cubs.

Finally, checking the speedometer, the SOD man stopped. Assuming Father Martinelli's Intel was correct, he guessed they were between five to ten kilometers northeast of the slave-labor camp. Under the light of a half-moon and a velvet sky twinkling with myriad stars, the Hangman and his white troop hopped out of the Land Rover. Quickly, they hacked out a section of brush. Hangman moved the Land Rover off the road, and his soldiers buried the vehicle with brush and vines.

NVD goggles in place, silencers attached to their Uzis, black greasepaint smeared over their faces, the Hangman and his three white dogs of war moved off into the jungle. Hangman ordered Schnell to walk point. Swiftly, silently, they moved, becoming one with the jungle and the stygian darkness. Politics, history, and the betterment of international relations now aside, they were all business.

Deadly business.

A killing trade.

They wended their way up a steep trail, using the ridge of a high hill as a landmark to bear down on. Beyond the hill, Hangman made out the clank and grind of hydraulic machinery and power shovels, the metallic groan of conveyor belts. At the foot of the hill, the Hangman and his soldiers gave the ridge a quick but thorough surveillance through infrared high-powered binocs. Satisfied that there were no sentries, the specialist led his cutthroats up the hill. As he neared the top of the hill, Hangman made out the thin beams of light that knifed into the sky.

When he topped the hill, the Hangman spotted those sources of light. And he found the slave-labor camp. A death camp, too.

Twelve-foot-high barbed-wire fences surrounded the diamond field. The diamond field itself was set on a rocky, sandswept plateau deep in the bowels of the valley.

Schnell, White, and Williams flanked the Hangman, spread out in prone positions along the ridge. All of them took in the activity below through their field glasses.

Occasionally, the sound of a whip lashing flesh, a cry of pain knifed the humid Congo night. True to what Martinelli had told them, Hangman discovered the horror that had taken Zaire by storm. A Fourth Reich storm.

Dozens of white men, armed with what the

Hangman guessed were Belgian FN-LARS or West German HK91s, patrolled the diamond field. Kleig lights bathed the grounds. Watchtowers were positioned at all points around the labor camp. Searchlights raked the sprawling grounds and the black surrounding hills. But it was the swastika on each watchtower that caught the Hangman's eye for a moment. No, he thought, this wasn't any human rights movement.

Then he saw the half-dozen bodies entangled in the barbed wire. He counted three generators near the long rows of wooden quarters, guessed that those generators also juiced the fence.

Black holes at the foot of the hills to the west, north, and south led to the "blue grounds." Frequent rumbles washed out of those poorly lit maws to the underground mines. Dynamite blasting. To the south, huge rotary scoops dug at the sand, searching to expose the diamond-bearing gravels that lay perhaps sixty to a hundred feet below the surface. Carts rolled on tracks to and from the mines. Black workers pushed the carts across the field toward the train tracks. The train tracks ran directly below the Hangman's position and wound through the hills to the north. Crushed diamond blue ground was hauled in carts from the mines, shoveled onto conveyor belts that rolled for the recovery plant to the northwest.

What the Hangman supposed were fuel and arms depots sat at the north end of the mine field garrison. Two black helicopter gunships were also parked near the north wall. From all appearances, there wasn't a white man who did a lick of manual labor. The whites were the ones with the assault rifles.

A three-round stutter of automatic-weapons fire rang out across the compound. Hangman and his troops looked to one of the mine entrances. There, a Fourth Reicher stood over a black worker, his assault rifle barking. The worker twitched for a second, then went limp. The neo-Nazi kicked the body, wheeled, strode back into the mine.

None of the Hangman's troops said a word.

Finally, Mac White spoke. "Looks like we might need some air-fire support from Spectre on this one, Cap'n. What do you think?"

The numbers were big, yeah. But the Hangman wanted a closer look. It looked as if the storage bins along the tracks were being loaded. The destination of that shipment might tell him something, perhaps lead them all to the head of the Fourth Reich hydra.

Hangman checked his Seiko. 0523.

"What next, Sarge?"

"We wait," he told Williams, "for the train to roll in."

And they didn't have to wait long.

A little more than an hour after the first light of dawn broke over the jungle, the train rolled in from the south. A big, lumbering wood-and-iron behemoth. Perhaps two hundred black workers were rounded up by fifty neo-Nazis and ushered to the cargo areas. Angry shouts and threats bellowed from the mouths of the Fourth Reichers. Black workers began loading the cars.

"Looks like our ticket to ride," the Hangman told his troops. Crouched low, he moved out along the ridge. To the northeast, he spotted a ledge of tree-covered rimrock that hung out over the tracks.

Next port of call, the Hangman thought, Hotel Destiny.

Or a bon voyage to the River Styx.

CHAPTER EIGHT

Herbert Schnell dropped the liver into the specimen jar. He was tired. Tired of the memory of a dream that had died many years ago. Tired of living in the past.

Tired of his life.

How many had they killed at Auschwitz? A million? Two million? Had he merely been a tool, bought and sold, used as part of the climate of a cultural insanity?

Mengele, he thought. The Angel of Death had once told him and the other twenty-one camp doctors not to view their work at Auschwitz as "systematic killing," but to see themselves as racial scientists weeding the defectives from the breeding stock. It was medical science, Mengele had said. Euthanasia clearly meant a stronger, superior Germany. Defectives in the species were just dead weight that would eventually drag down the strong, he had said.

Yom Kippur, Schnell recalled, was always a special day at Auschwitz. The SS troops would round up the Jewish boys for selection by the camp doctors. The Jews would recite a prayer on their Day of Atonement, believing they were the flock that passed beneath the rod of the shepherd. And their Lord would decide who would live.

Who would live. Who would die. Who would be marked for dissection.

The faces of the small children as they walked, naked, to the showers to be gassed still haunted him. He hadn't slept well in more than forty years, and even with a heavy dose of barbiturates, his sleep was restless, tormented. At night, the faces—torn, twisted, flesh dripping as it sizzled off the skulls of Jews—boiled through his dreams. And during the day, it was as if the memory of the past night's visions of Hell lived inside of him. Voices crying. Imploring him. *"Why?"* they asked.

He had no answer. He just stood there, frozen in disbelief.

The sign above the gates of Auschwitz, he recalled, had read *Arbeit Macht Frei.* Work makes you free. The horror of that reality for the Jews had been *Death makes you free.* For many Jews, he thought, death had been a blessing, preferable to going under his knife. At Auschwitz, he and his brother had experimented on thousands of live subjects. Removing organs. Sewing up the subjects, then waiting to see how long they lived without a liver, or kidneys, or intestines. Cutting open major arteries, or castrating males. Watching the blood run. Monitoring the time it took a subject to bleed to death. Removing sections of skull, wiring areas of the brain to electrodes. Bodies strapped to water-slick metal tables, convulsing with each jolt of electricity. In his mind, he saw the youthful, unlined face of Herbert Schnell. A calm face, an impassive stare. Detached. Alone. A giant in the midst of controlled madness.

Only a last-minute bribe had gotten both him

and his brother out of Poland. But now it all seemed to be starting again.

The dream was dead. But the nightmare lived on.

But Herbert Schnell was tired.

Tired of living.

But afraid of dying.

In death, he feared, he would have to face the millions. He would have to face the children.

He was one of the damned, like Mengele. He could feel it deep inside. A cold, gnawing fear.

Turning, Schnell walked back to the metal table. There, his Bakongo subject was strapped down. A gag was stuffed into the black man's mouth. Schnell had removed the man's liver while he was awake, as he had always operated on his subjects.

Quickly, mechanically, he attached the wire heads. He felt like a man walking through his own dream as he moved to the source of the electrode. He flipped on the switch, and violently, his subject convulsed, blood gushing from the hole in his stomach as lethal voltage sizzled his flesh.

It was over.

And as he always had, he went to the sink, removed his surgical gloves, and dropped them in a wastebasket. For a full minute he scrubbed his hands with soap and disinfectant, then dipped his hands into a bowl of rubbing alcohol.

"Brother."

Startled, Herbert Schnell turned. Alois, standing tall and proud with his SS cap on, smiled at him from the doorway. How, he asked himself, could he tell his brother how damned sick and tired he felt? He only wanted to be far, far away from this place. He only wanted to forget, finish out his life in quiet solitude. Detached from the past. Living only in the moment.

"You do not look well, Herbert. Is something troubling you?"

"*Nein.*" He lied to his older brother.

"*Gut.* Because we must be ready. The time has

come, brother. We begin to make our move. Our black puppets are ready to be put into power in Cape Town and Pretoria. Our followers await their instructions now in the Transvaal. The assassinations, the revolution, will begin immediately. There is no time to waste. It seems complications have arisen."

"Complications?"

Alois Schnell shook his head slowly. "No need for you to worry about them. Everything is under my control."

His brother's scheme for South African conquest was madness, Herbert Schnell knew. Doomed before the first batch of nerve gas was even sprayed over the black homelands in Johannesburg. It didn't matter how many white dissidents in important positions inside the government and the Army he had bought. Just what was his brother thinking, anyway? They would slaughter tens of thousands. It would work, *ja*, for a while. They had some power. They had some backing.

But they were doomed to fail. He could feel that in his heart, too.

How? Why had their long, nomadic postwar flight from German and Israeli vengeance-hunters led them here?

"We will seize the reins of power," Alois Schnell said, "as soon as the white minority in the RSA sees the black revolution upon them. Of course, the whites will have to fight back. But they will find their armies and their police force have turned against them. They will all have to come to us to save themselves. They will get no help from the outside once the world knows the RSA has gassed several of the homelands. We, brother, hold the final, the only solution. Come," he snapped, wheeling. "I want to see how effectively the nerve gas works."

Schnell followed his brother out into the corridor. They walked down a long metal plank deep in the abandoned mine shaft. Generator-powered lights hung from the craggy rock walls. The gangway overlooked a large cavern dug out by hydraulic machinery. Hundreds of black drums filled this area. Brown-uniformed soldiers with assault rifles guarded the drums.

Within moments, the notorious Surgeons of the SS were standing in front of a Plexiglas cubicle. Father McMillan and Nambala stood against the far wall inside the cubicle. Anger and hatred blazed in the black chieftain's eyes. Fear masked McMillan.

Alois Schnell gave one of his troopers a curt nod. The trooper flicked a switch on a panel hung over a black drum.

Alois Schnell clasped his hands behind his back. Herbert Schnell's gaze narrowed. Moments later, the invisible, deadly vapor took effect.

"Instant paralysis of the respiratory and nervous systems," Alois Schnell commented, watching as the two doomed men went ramrod-stiff, flattening against the wall. Their mouths vented, tongues protruded. The whites of McMillan's eyes showed as they rolled back in his head.

"Less than a teaspoonful," Alois Schnell said. "Volatilized. Death within seconds. *Gut.* It is ready."

He said this with no more emotion than if he were reading from an itinerary.

Herbert Schnell felt his brother's eyes boring into him.

"I have ordered every village razed by fire," he said. "The gas is being readied now on the gunships." Schnell's throaty laugh sounded hollow as it rang through the cave. "The purifying extermination of inferiors, you understand."

"*Ja,* I understand, Alois," he said, then cursed himself for his cowardice, his weakness in being unable to stand up to his brother.

Alois Schnell smiled. He looked inside the cubicle.

Father McMillan and Nambala dropped to the floor.

"Fisherman."

Jackson plunged the tip of the Kukri into the ground. His back braced against the side of the hut, he looked up and met Barnes's surly expression.

"You seen Walker?"

Jackson laughed. "Hell, seen him? The whole village has 'seen' him, bro."

Barnes felt his anger rising as he stared down at the black fisherman. "What are you talkin' about, man?"

"Niar. That li'l ole sugar baby, bro. Ain't that what you're talkin' about?" Jackson chuckled, drawing in the dirt with his Kukri. "Looked to me like the hitter had the same thing on his mind that you do. He's been followin' that little girl around since the crack of dawn. Nose just all wrinkled up like he's some bloodhound." He laughed.

Barnes looked around the village. The sun, clear now of the tree line, burned down on the huts. Women walked up and down the path that led to the river, urns atop their heads. Fires boiled beneath pots. Men skinned fish or carried mud bricks to the kiln to be seasoned for hut construction. Bashongo boys unfurled grass nets, ran wild through the village. Zumba, decked out in leopard skin, sat in front of a fire near the doorway to his hut. The witch doctor wore about four layers of animal teeth around his neck. Solemnly, he stared into the fire.

Barnes looked toward Niar's hut. No sign of anyone there. Shit, he thought. Be just like Walker to try and score the only nice-looking pussy in town. All the other village women, the black street assassin thought, were either too old, too ugly, too fat, or had scarred their flesh long ago with the stupid tribal adornment. Hitter or no hitter, if Walker was trying to fuck Niar, Barnes decided he'd have something to say about it.

"Hey, man," Jackson said, showing Barnes a crooked grin. "You two better back off a little. Hell, we know the girl's old man was taken away to that camp sometime back, like the good Father told us. And I'm sure she's aching to have it just as much as you, blood. But the padre," he said, pointing with the Kukri toward the group of village children gathered around Martinelli near his hut. "He might take offense to a little fornicatin'."

Barnes strode away from Jackson and growled, "You're beginning to look mighty white to me, fisherman."

Frowning, Jackson watched as Barnes walked toward Niar's hut and thrust open the door.

Walker rolled off Niar. Jumping up off the grass bed, he snatched up his pants. Furious, he stared at Barnes for a moment, then rasped, "What you want, man? Why don't you knock next time. Better yet, mind your own fucking business."

Barnes stood in the doorway, found himself speechless, paralyzed for some reason. He wasn't sure why he'd barged in on Walker and Niar. A wild impulse? Jealousy? Rage knotted his guts as he stood in the humiliation that he had brought on himself. But he had listened to enough shit already from the white boys. He wasn't going to take any more shit. From anybody.

"Hey, blood," Barnes said, "you ain't gotta talk to me like I was one of them."

Niar sat up, drawing her knees to her chest. Her dark eyes, the color of rich chocolate, were wide with fear.

"One of what?" Walker growled.

"One of the white dudes."

Walker took a menacing step toward Barnes. The chiseled muscles in his bare chest and arms flexed, seemed to rip, swell. Air rasped out of the nostrils of his broad, flat nose. He squared his broad shoulders, looked Barnes dead in the eye. Murder was in the rumble of his low-pitched voice as he told Barnes,

"Let me tell you something, nigger. I've listened to you whine about a whole lot of shit since I laid eyes on you. Black power this, white motherfucker that. All you been whinin' about is the shit you made out of your own life, nigger. You ain't nothin' to me. *Nothin'*. You're less to me than those white fuckers. Around me you ain't shit, 'cause you're just another smart-mouthed nigger boy, and don't you forget it. Ever."

Barnes looked at Walker for a moment in disbelief. He felt the adrenaline burn, rushing into his blood. Hatred seized him. He threw thirty-odd years of bad, ugly feeling behind the right fist. The sweeping blow cracked like thunder off Walker's jaw. The ex-heavyweight stumbled back. Barnes followed Walker across the room, drilling a left, then a right across the ex-heavy's jaw.

But it was like pounding stone with a fork.

Walker's rage exploded. Spinning like a cyclone, he whipped his fist across Barnes's face, snapping the Harlem hit man's head sideways. The ex-heavy followed up with a piled-driving uppercut, burying a right fist deep into Barnes's gut. Doubled over, Barnes dropped to his knees. As Walker raised both hands over his head to deliver a neck-breaking blow, Barnes drilled a fist into the ex-heavy's nuts.

Sucking the air as if he had a hole in his lung, Barnes clambered to his feet. He staggered back toward the open doorway like a drunk. Thick red blood dribbled over his lower lip. His senses reeling, he started to turn toward Walker.

The rampaging bull that was Walker blasted headfirst into Barnes's midsection. Flesh and bone thudded like a punching bag dropped on the ground from a ten-story window. Walker and Barnes exploded through the branch wall, slammed to the ground. Dust boiled over the two black men as they grappled with each other, fighting to clutch some vital point, struggling to get a death grip on the other's neck.

Bashongo boys broke from Martinelli's circle. They ran toward the brawl, laughing, shouting encouragement to the combatants in Bantu.

"Stop them! Stop them!" Martinelli yelled at Jackson.

The black fisherman stood and looked from Martinelli to the tangle of arms and legs that was Walker and Barnes.

"Stop them this minute!"

Jackson took several steps toward the fight but stopped. Shit, he thought, those two brothers meant business. No way he was sticking his neck in that. Four hundred pounds of black fury would kick his ass clear across the Congo, he told himself.

Walker rolled on top of Barnes. The ex-heavy raised his fist to smash Barnes's face in. Barnes, sliding his foot up, plunged his boot into Walker's gut, driving the ex-heavy away from him. Jumping to his feet, Barnes hammered a vicious right roundhouse across Walker's eye, splitting skin.

Jackson shrugged at Martinelli. "No way, Father. No way, man."

Barnes cracked a roundhouse kick off Walker's jaw. Walker, seemingly unfazed, threw all two hundred and twenty-five pounds into a right that caught Barnes on the jaw, nearly ripping his head off his shoulders. Barnes spun with the impact and slammed to the ground on his side.

The children cheered Walker as the ex-heavy, blood streaming down the side of his face, straightened. He waited to see if Barnes was down for the count.

The Harlem hit man wasn't about to throw in the towel. His head felt as if it had been split open by a sledgehammer, yeah, but renewed strength was fed by a powerful hatred. Slowly, he climbed to his feet.

Walker took a step toward Barnes, lifting clenched fists. Barnes circled, took a step forward, and snapped three straight rights off Walker's chin with lightning speed. Barnes drew his right arm

back, craned a knockout blow for Walker's dome.
But the ex-heavy threw his arm out, blocking the
blow. Instantly, he snaked his right arm beneath
Barnes's armpit. His arm wrapped around Barnes's
upper back, Walker threw his hip into the Harlem
killer's stomach. Weight shifted, knees bent, he
flipped Barnes over his head, driving him into the
ground.

Suddenly, women charged into the village from
the river path. Water sloshed out of urns, the jugs
falling to the ground. Panicked cries ripped from
their mouths.

Stretched on his side, Barnes swung his arm
around like a whip. Driving his arm into Walker's
leg, he bowled the ex-heavy down. Through the
blood in his eyes, Barnes noticed the villagers scattering as they bolted toward the huts. He looked at
Walker as the ex-heavy rolled onto his side, Jackson
and the Italian priest running toward him.

"What the hell . . ." Walker rumbled.

"You dudes done bangin' each other around?"
Jackson rasped breathlessly, throwing an Uzi down
in front of Barnes. "We got incoming. Gunships.
And they ain't ours."

Blood dripping off his jaw, Walker pushed himself
up onto his hands and knees. Barnes looked up. A
moment later, the tree line began to wave.

Barnes jumped to his feet, cursing.

Walker snatched the MM-1 out of Jackson's hand.

CHAPTER NINE

Crouching, the Hangman broke cover from behind the brush, swiftly leading the others across the ledge as the train thundered beneath them. He gauged the distance to the train roof, timed his jump, and leapt from the ledge. He dropped four feet, hitting the top of a car on his side. Grunting, the air driven from his lungs, he rolled, Uzi jabbing viciously into his ribs. He came to a stop inches from the back edge of the car, staring down at the coupling and the tracks that blurred by. Lifting his head, he saw Williams, Schnell, and White hit the roofs two and three cars back. As he had ordered, they remained outstretched until the train was a good kilometer beyond the diamond field and the roving eyes of watchtower guards.

Once out of sight, Hangman pulled himself into a crouch. Silenced Uzi in hand, he signaled the others. Schnell knelt near the edge of the train while Williams and White jogged toward the caboose, leaping from roof to roof.

The wood vibrating beneath his boots, Hangman moved back to the edge of the car. As he looked down, a narrow iron gangway slid out and dropped beneath the doors to each car. Seconds later, a half-dozen brown-uniformed soldiers toting HK91s and wearing swastika armbands stepped out onto the gangway, moving in the direction of the caboose. One Nazi trained his assault rifle on the opening to the trailing car while the other slid the door back. Checking for stowaways. Smart, the Hangman thought. Within moments, that search paid off for the neo-Nazis. Automatic-weapons fire rang out. Hangman peered over the edge as a bloody, bullet-riddled black body was tossed away from the train.

As the specialist looked to the engine cab, he saw an SS cap poke up over the edge. *What the hell?* It was possible that someone had seen them jump, but unlikely. No, this must be another routine spot check.

Quickly, the CIA assassin moved toward the cab. Smoke belched from the engine's stack—a dark, ugly smudge against a bright blue early morning sky. Black clouds swept over the Hangman as he vaulted from car to car.

The SS guy wasn't aware of the green-eyed invader until he topped the last rung of his ladder. It was his tough luck. The Hangman exploded a roundhouse kick off the side of the neo-Nazi's head. Sailing off the train, the guy followed his assault rifle and SS cap down into the ravine. A bone-breaking trip to the concentration camp along the River Styx. Hangman looked down through the open, narrow window to the engine cab. Driver, fireman, and gunner. The gunner was working on a cigarette, and all three neo-Nazis seemed oblivious to their comrade's sudden departure. Not so for a Hitlerian on the gangway.

Thunder in his ears, burning coal exhaust stinging his nose, the SOD assassin moved back toward the rear of the train. Williams and Schnell were in kill-positions, but White was nowhere to be seen. Glancing over the edge, Hangman saw a brown-uniformed body, arms windmilling, assault rifle flying from his hands, tumble down the steep hillside. The ex-Klansman at work, Hangman knew. The guy had shown some initiative, but he'd also thrown a bucketful of shit into the fan.

Hangman unleashed his Uzi on the Nazis below him. Two guys looked up; two faces were obliterated by 9mm slugs burping from the SMG's snout. Grabbing the iron frame of a ladder, Hangman dropped down over the edge of the roof. Triggering the Israeli subgun one-handed, he stitched a neo-Nazi from assbone, up the spine, and opened the back of the Fourth Reicher's skull with the gory end of his barrage. Bloody chunks of bone and brain followed the SS cap and its dead owner off the train.

As Hangman hit the gangway, a peal of thunder sounded two cars down. Looking up, he saw a brown-uniformed sack of Nazi garbage propelled away from the roof. He caught a half-second glimpse of the wound canal in the neo-Nazis's chest. A wound canal the size of a basketball. Hangman cursed the German merc. The sonofabitch just couldn't let go of that fucking SPAS. Any more bullshit out of Schnell on this operation and he decided he'd dock the German the next time out. Not in money. Hell, no. He'd take away Schnell's autoshotgun kill-toy.

Hangman then saw Schnell appear at the roof's edge, SPAS pointing down, raking the gangway for another target.

As White loped down the gangway, a neo-Nazi swung out of the caboose, HK91 drawing a bead on the ex-Klansman's back. Schnell and Williams took that Hitlerian out with a combined Uzi spray and SPAs blast. A piece of partially decapitated, shredded neo-Nazi meat was kicked away from the gangway as if jerked back by an invisible fist.

Quickly, as Schnell and Williams guarded their

backsides from the roof, Hangman and White checked each car for neo-Nazi guns. There were none. But the specialist and the ex-Klansman found piles of crates and burlap sacks draped over by swastika banners in each car.

"What's the plan now, Cap'n?"

"We ride this train out."

"Might've helped if we could've taken some uniforms, huh? Get us inside of wherever the end of the ride is."

Hangman ignored White and moved toward the crates in the boxcar.

"You thinkin' what I'm thinkin' might be in those boxes?"

Hangman stood over the burlap sacks. "Call Schnell and Williams down."

White stepped out onto the gangway and whistled up at Schnell and Williams. Moments later, the one-eyed pirate and the German merc stepped into the car behind Hangman and White.

With his Fairbairn-Sykes, Hangman sliced through a swastika, gutting open a fat burlap sack. Diamonds tumbled onto the wooden floor of the boxcar.

Mac White's eyes widened. "Holy..."

The SPAS slowly lowered to Schnell's side, his blue eyes glittering behind hooded lids.

Williams unsheathed his Kukri. He swept a swastika banner off a crate. With the Kukri's blade, he pried up the top of the crate and ripped it off. "Jesus, look at this. Look at this!"

Hangman looked, all right. Bars of solid gold gleamed at the one-eyed pirate.

"You reckon this is maybe somebody's big payoff, Cap'n?" White laughed. "One of the spear-chuckers in Mobutu's government?"

The three Death Row soldiers ripped open burlap sacks with their commando daggers. With wild glee, they emptied the sacks, flooding the floorboard with diamonds, rubies, pearls.

Williams began stuffing a sack with diamonds and bars of gold. The one-eyed killer couldn't cram diamonds into the sack fast enough. "I knew this trip was gonna pay off, Sarge. Man-o-man! I just fucking knew it. I love it! I love you! I love all you fuckers!" he shouted, hurling a handful of diamonds into the air.

"Don't think our Nazi buddies'll mind spreading a little of the wealth around, do you, Cap'n? Christ! There's enough gems here to make us king of the fuckin' mountain for life!"

"Yeah, man!" Williams whooped. "Vegas, here I come. Atlantic City, watch out. Bel Air, baby, yeah. Big fucking mansion. Cadillac convertible. They'll love this white boy's ass in L.A. I'll be fuckin' about three inches off my cock the first week there."

Hangman took a long step toward Williams as the one-eyed pirate stood, slinging the sack over his shoulder. The SOD man lashed a backhand hammer fist across Williams's jaw. The sudden, cracking blow and the weight of the gems on his back dropped Williams to the floorboard.

White and Schnell froze. Anger blazed into Williams's lone eye as he wiped the blood off his lip.

There was ice in the Hangman's voice as he warned all three men, "Any of you greedy shitheads tries to leave here with one diamond, one bar of gold, you won't make it out of this jungle alive. I'll see to that personally. Now, I hate to be a tough guy. Hell, nobody hates having to be tough guy more than me, but—"

Williams looked past Hangman.

His eyes locked on the back of the Hangman's head, Mac White carefully picked his Uzi up off the floorboard.

Hangman cocked his head. "Suggestion, pal. Don't try it."

A nervous smile flickered over White's lips. He lifted the Uzi another inch. "Hey, Cap'n, c'mon. Lighten up some, man. What the hell would it hurt, huh? A sackful for each of us. Whatever happened to the spoils of war?"

Hangman kept his face at right angles to White and Schnell. Adrenaline pumped like fire through his veins. "This war's not over," the SOD man said. "And you don't want me as an enemy, White. Believe it."

White's voice was low-pitched, dangerous. "I believe you, Cap'n. Hell, I wouldn't fuck with you for all the diamonds in Africa."

Hangman saw the Uzi come up another inch. He would kill White if he had to. He would kill all three of them, without hesitation, without remorse. One more inch, he told himself, and he would drive his heel into White's nose, plunging bone into the ex-Klansman's brain.

Suddenly, a thunderous explosion rocked the train. Gunfire erupted beyond the car. A series of tremendous blasts sent shock waves through the boxcar, knocking the Hangman and his soldiers to the floorboard.

Pushing himself to his feet, the Hangman led the way to the door, the others flanking him.

"Who the hell are those guys?" White breathed.

Fifty meters ahead, a large paramilitary unit descended on an unidentified outpost. Hangman watched as brown-uniformed soldiers went down under the spray of Uzi subgun fire. Two dozen soldiers in light gray uniforms surged down the hills flanking the tracks while SMG fire covered them from above. A geysering fireball suddenly vaporized the outpost, hurtling two Land Rovers across the tracks like scraps of flying junk. Rocket fire then streaked from the jungle.

"Shit!" White bellowed as HE projectiles impacted into the engine cab. "Balls to the wall!"

"Jump!" the Hangman yelled as the second and third cards were vomited from the tracks by pounding explosions.

The Hangman took the hill on his side, dust boiling over his face, choking his lungs. A horrible rending sounded above him as debris caromed off his head. White, Schnell, and Williams tumbled head over heels down the slope. Explosions ripped apart another car in a hurricane of fire and black smoke. Gems rained to the ground around the Hangman and his Death Row soldiers, and the SOD man felt a gold bar hammer into his leg. Wood and twisted iron wreckage shot into the sky as the strike force decimated the train with relentless rocket fire. Iron screeched a split second later as the back-end cars slowly tipped off to the side.

Leaping to his feet, the Hangman opened up on Nazis as they scrambled away from the outpost. The SOD man and his three killers hosed the fleeing Hitlerians with SMG fire, hammering SS flunkies to the ground as twitching red meat. Like some mortally wounded behemoth lying down to die, the pulverized train wreckage derailed in sections of two- and three-coupled cars. Clouds of brown smoke churned the air as the cars pounded down the hillside. Hangman and his soldiers ran for their lives as potentially crushing debris rolled after them. Clearing the explosions of wood, the showering waves of gold and diamonds, the Hangman and his soldiers took cover in the jungle.

Sporadic gunfire sounded near the outpost. Prisoners were being quickly executed by the mysterious strike force.

"Hold your fire!" Hangman yelled out to the commandos.

"You in there! Throw down your weapons! Come out with your hands up!"

"Do it," the SOD man ordered, looking at the numbers converging on the tracks and outpost. "I'd say they've got us outnumbered by about fifteen to one."

"I'd say you're smart," White allowed in a grumble.

After they tossed their weapons out into the

open, the Hangman and his soldiers stepped into the clearing. Hands atop their heads, they waited. Uzi-brandishing soldiers ran up to them.

They were white men. And, Hangman saw moments later, they wore armbands. The Star of David. Solomon's Seal, yeah. Six-pointed symbol of Judaism. *What the hell?* But it wasn't the time for a lot of questions, the specialist figured. They'd been caught with their pants down again.

"Jews," Schnell breathed.

"Shut up, German," Williams muttered.

Two tall, lean, dark-eyed, dark-haired men led the commandos. Within moments, the Hangman and his soldiers were surrounded by three dozen Uzis. Commandos stripped the four men of all weapons.

A Jewish commando with burning dark eyes stepped forward. For a long moment he regarded his captives with suspicion.

"Who are you?" he barked.

Hangman glanced around at the unwavering Uzi muzzles.

"CIA," he said, then cracked, "But don't tell anybody."

The commando lowered the Uzi by his side and snorted.

CHAPTER TEN

Leroy Walker tightened his grip on the MM-1. He moved into the doorway of Niar's hut, back braced against the mud jamb. Dust whirlpools gyrated down the middle of the village. He heard the staccato lashing of chopper blades. He felt the sweat run cold down his neck, smelled the stink of fear on his body. He trembled with a feverish adrenaline rush. He tasted the blood in his mouth, flowing freely from a lip that had been split wide during his brawl with Barnes.

Death, he knew, was going to take somebody.

Whoooooosh.

He peered around the corner, saw the giant tongue of fire turn a hut into a roiling ball of orange-red flames. Two gunships. Both set down at the far west end of the village. Across the street, he saw the fisherman lean into the doorjamb, pulling the pin on a grenade with his teeth. Damn, he thought. *Damn!* Just the three of them. Against how many? Hell, they had one advantage, Walker told himself.

Surprise.

And surprise them he did. As the Nazi gunners disembarked from the gunships, the ex-heavy-weight swung around, dropped to a knee, and un-leased the MM-1. Three hellfire rounds belched from Walker's squat, recoilless rocket launcher as Jackson lobbed an M15 thermite grenade. Four con-secutive ear-shattering detonations hurtled Nazis skyward in bits and shreds. Two of Walker's MM-1 HE rounds pulverized one of the black gunships. Slick-looking fireballs meshed, boiling away from splintering chopper wreckage, consuming Hitler-ians.

One Nazi writhed on the ground, slapping at the white phosphorus that had ignited his hair and masked his face in flames.

"Back to the ovens, you Nazi bastards!" Walker yelled, strapping on the MM-1, unslinging the At-chisson. Unholy *Motherfucker*, he suddenly thought. He was starting to think like the cracker. The big white bigot's battle cry of *Long live Israel,* as the cracker had mowed down or blown up about two dozen Muslim dungeaters and sent them to that Great Mosque in Hell, still rang in his ears from the first mission. Yeah, three fucking missions, the ex-heavyweight thought, and he was the cracker in blackface. *Shit!* Yeah, sure, he'd always seen any white dude as a bigoted, scared piece of shit that had just been in his way. Now, though, that narrow tunnel of bloodied vision took in a few more peoples of the world. Arab. Jew. Commie. Whitey. Chad. Dickhead. Shithead. Pukeface. Hell, the thing was, he was loving every last fucking second of it. Box the sonofabitch up. Label the cocksucker. It made killing somebody easier to live with. *Gimme a fuckin' piece and turn this nigger's ass loose, ba-beeeee!*

Nazis charging into the village from the second gunship found themselves caught in a scissoring crossfire hurricane.

Barnes, Uzi blazing, scythed six "brown-uniforms' with an entire magazine of 9mm lead as the black street assassin cut into the enemy numbers from their rear. The Nazis had come expecting an easy slaughter. What they got instead was a black tornado of bloody, lightning death.

Walker's autoshotgun pounded out twelve-bore flesh-shredders and skull-erupters. As the ex-heavyweight swept over the decimated Nazi numbers with full-auto Atchisson butchery, Jackson cleaned up with a hailstorm of 9mm slugs. Muzzling at 420 meters per second, the Parabellum tumblers thwacked off chunks of flesh, sending Nazis corkscrewing to the ground, flailing back into the fire.

Slapping a fresh thirty-two-round clip home, Barnes bounded into the gunship's fuselage. "Freeze, motherfucker!" he shouted at the pilot.

The pilot was smart.

The copilot played it stupid.

As he twisted around in his seat, the copilot triggered a three-round burst. Slugs whining off the roof above his head, Barnes flinched, then cut loose with his Uzi. The copilot's helmet disintegrated in large hunks. Larger hunks of skullbone disintegrated, too, and globs of brain matter splattered the Plexiglas.

"Try something stupid, asshole!" Barnes savagely rasped, sounding almost as if he were inviting the guy to punch his own ticket. "You'll be wearin' your brains on the glass like him."

Walker and Jackson swept through the sheeting black smoke, the wavering walls of fire. Side by side, weapons roaring, the ex-heavyweight and the Florida fisherman pulped wounded Nazis, hammering their remains into the dusty soil.

Before boarding the gunship, Walker looked back

at the kill-zone. An arm twitched nearby, behind a veil of oily smoke. Walker triggered the Atchisson, ending the twitching.

Jackson stumbled into the fuselage. The fisherman slumped against the wall, breathless, a slick sweat coating his face.

"Get this bitch up, Nazi!" Walker growled, moving beside Barnes. "Back to base. Any shit, any shit at all, I'll fly this bitch myself."

The Nazi fly-boy grumbled an oath but reached for the Collective stick.

The Nazi warbird lifted off.

"What the hell we gonna do?" Jackson demanded.

"We're goin' in, fisherman," Walker replied.

"What?"

Walker addressed the anxiety in Jackson's eyes with an icy glare. "Get your head outta your ass, fisherman. I said we're goin' in."

"That means it's our ballgame," Barnes added.

Jackson shook his head. "You brothers is nuts."

"When you gonna smarten up, nigger?" Walker growled. "We're on our own. Just like it's been from the beginning. Just like it'll be until we buy a piece of real estate here."

"You mean we're gonna take on the Fourth Reich? Just us?"

Walker's smile was pure defiance. "You're gettin' smarter by the second."

Jackson stared at the swollen, blood-caked faces of Walker and Barnes in disbelief. Finally, he shook his head, crooked a smile, shrugged. "What the hell . . ."

The combined West German–Israeli Nazi-hunters sifted through the debris of the kill-zone. Gold bars, gems, and weaponry were rounded up and piled near the train wreckage. The bodies of dead South African Nazis were strung out near the jungle brush. Hangman watched as commandos

placed gold Stars of David on the enemy dead. A
vengeance ritual, yeah, he decided. According to the
guerrilla leaders and brothers Abraham and Ruben
Husseini, it was a ritual fully justified by the stran-
gest, blackest time in history that the Jewish people
and a good part of the world had suffered through.
No, the Hangman thought, mankind had never wit-
nessed a darker time than what happened in Europe from 1921 through 1945. And, yeah, these
Jewish commandos had every right to their vengeance under the Star of David.

Following the firefight, the Hangman and the
commando brothers had exchanged information.
There was no point, the Hangman decided, in hiding any part of his search-and-destroy operation
from the brothers Husseini. They were soldiers on
the same side, fighting the same evil. The Husseinis
agreed with him. So the Nazi-hunters had returned
their weapons. And both sides had pledged to rid
the Dark Continent of the Fourth Reich scourge together.

The Husseinis had been tracking Nazi war criminals since the early '50s. They had taken an active
part in the hunt and capture of one Klaus Barbie,
alias Klaus Altmann. There had been no joy for
them in the capture of the Butcher of Lyons, they
said. For there would be no rest for them until
every last living Nazi was brought back to Israel,
tried, and convicted for his crimes against humanity before a people who had lost more than six million of their race to the Holocaust.

The Hangman took a cigarette break with the
Husseinis. As the cleanup continued around them,
the Hangman and the Husseinis sat down on
wreckage near the tracks. Schnell, the SOD man
noted, stuck close to his heels, lingering just a few
feet away from him. There was a new coldness
about the German, the Hangman sensed. A deep,
fearful loathing for something or someone. He could
never tell what the German was thinking or what

he would do next. But whatever went on inside his head, he knew, was not for the innocent or the faint of heart. In light of new developments, he was very suspicious now of what motivated the German mercenary. Wisely, Schnell was keeping his mouth shut, and the Hangman intended to do the same about the mercenary as far as his connection with the Nazi Surgeons was concerned. Quickly, he looked for White and Williams. White loitered near the jungle, working on a Camel. There was no sign of Williams.

"Where's Williams?" Hangman asked White.

The ex-Klansman shrugged, looking around. "Dunno. Said he went to take a dump."

"Keep an eye on that guy."

Ruben Husseini drew thoughtfully on his cigarette. There was a bar of gold between his feet. FAL, HK G-3, and R-4 automatic rifles had been piled beside him. He looked at the hardware and commented, "South African military firepower. It would seem Mossad Intelligence was correct. The heart of the Fourth Reich conspiracy is somewhere in the Republic." He shook his head ruefully and muttered, "Damn."

The Husseinis and their commandos, the Hangman had learned, were a covert unit combining agents from West Germany's Federal Center for Nazi War Criminals and specialists from Mossad's own branch of Special Operations. The Israelis, Hangman knew, had a lot more tolerance, gave a lot more support to covert counterterrorist teams than did Uncle Sam. They had to. The survival of an entire nation depended on their fighting strength. The Israeli military and Intelligence got free rein from their countrymen. In the States, he thought, the fucking politicians had the whole system handcuffed.

Abraham Husseini spoke up. He looked the Hangman dead in the eye with grim conviction. "Despite my brother's feelings, I am very much tempted to ask you and your commandos to stay out of this. This, my friend, should be entirely our struggle. A fight for the Jewish people and the State of Israel. You, my CIA friend, were not there at Auschwitz. You, my friend, did not bury the hundreds, the thousands of my people in open pits. You cannot even begin to imagine the horror." Husseini began to tremble.

The hell, the nightmare that was this man's past, was clearly, hauntingly visible in the Jew's eyes to the Hangman.

"We were *sonderkommandos*," brother Ruben explained, his voice quiet, more controlled than his brother's, but still on the verge of cracking with emotion. "We were perhaps ten years old when the Nazis came and took us from the Warsaw Ghetto. I can remember it as if it were only yesterday. At Treblinka, the Nazis forced all the Jews to strip. Mind you, it was thirty degrees below zero. They forced our mother to strip us. Our sister began to cry. A Nazi shouted at our mother several times to 'shut the child up.' Finally, he grabbed our sister from our mother's arms and smashed her head against a wall. Repeatedly, he did this. Then, as if she were some piece of garbage, he handed our dead sister back to our mother. She was three years old."

Christ, the Hangman thought. He felt a lump rise in his throat. He couldn't hold Husseini's dark, murderous stare.

Abraham Husseini bowed his head, squeezed his eyes shut. With his thumb and forefinger, he pinched the bridge of his nose. His knuckles turned stark white.

There was a long moment of hard silence.

Hangman saw a silent tear roll down Abraham Husseini's cheek.

"Imagine this, my friend," Ruben Husseini said, "and you will understand our anger. You will understand why we are a race that stands alone. Alone, yes, but not out of choice. Think then, my friend, about apartheid in South Africa. There are some real and very frightening similarities."

Hangman looked away from Husseini. Christ, he felt for the guy. He tried to steady the shaking in his hand as he drew on his cigarette butt. *God in Heaven.* Just what the hell had really gone on inside the heads of those Nazi monsters, he had to wonder.

No one in this life would ever really know for sure.

Or even understand why.

But Hangman had his own war to fight now.

CHAPTER ELEVEN

Leroy Walker wasn't concerned about consequences. He wanted some action. Results, too. With a feeling of grim, concrete resolve, the ex-heavyweight replaced the three spent HE loads in the MM-1. Next to the Atchisson, he found himself growing very fond of this weird-looking rocket launcher. It had a way of making him into a one-man army in one hell of a hurry. This bitch could hurl twelve rounds in five seconds. During the two weeks' training for Operation Apocalypse, he must've blown up five square miles of mock targets and compounds with the MM-1. The cracker would've taken his MM-1 to bed with him at night if the Hangman had let him. Yeah, firepower. Lots of it.

Firepower Walker.

He liked the sound of that.

And, hell yes, Walker decided, if the three of them worked together, they wouldn't have any problem taking out the Nazi garrison by themselves. *Fuck the white guys*.

Walker, rotor wash slapping his face, became painfully aware of his battered features. He touched his split lip, spat out a mouthful of blood. Yeah, he still had a score to settle with the Harlem nigger. And he didn't intend to let the next time go past the opening bell. The brother wasn't a bad hitter, though, he had to admit to himself. But Barnes was slow to follow up with the right. And he had a way of leaving himself open with the left. Wasn't much on body shots, either. Always went for the KO. Walker made a mental note to go for a gutshot next time.

"Hey, man, we got somethin' comin' up."

Walker turned and looked at the fisherman. He walked to the cockpit. Two hundred meters to the north, the diamond field came into sight.

"That it?" Barnes demanded of the pilot.

The pilot stayed belligerently silent until Barnes jabbed him in the rib with the Uzi.

"Yeah, that's it."

Judging by his thick accent, Walker thought the pilot was British, but the rotor whine and the wind whipping through the open fuselage door distorted sound. And he'd never talked to a Dutchman in his life. He just wanted to get it straight in his mind what this guy was before he killed him.

"Fly past it!"

Jackson looked at Walker, confused. "Say what?"

"I don't trust this Nazi-lovin' fucker," the ex-heavyweight snarled. "Fly around it, man. Now! Or you're dead shit."

The pilot hesitated.

"You heard him," Barnes rasped, jabbing his Uzi's muzzle into the guy's ribs. "And don't touch nothin' on that panel unless I tell ya."

As the Nazi pilot banked to the east, Walker moved back to the doorway. He couldn't see the activity down on the mine field. But he'd seen the dead blacks hanging in the barbed-wire walls. And, hell yes, he could just imagine the rest. Whips flaying black backs and shoulders. Beatings. Shootings. Slave labor. African blacks, he thought, doing all the dirty work while Whitey got rich off their blood and sweat. Barnes, he knew, wasn't too far off when he started bellyaching about his nigger's misfortune. Walker just didn't like to see it, or hear it, from that one. He didn't need to have a mirror held up to his own deep-seated boiling rage all the time. He didn't need to be reminded all the time of his own dead end in life.

"What's the plan?"

Walker turned toward Jackson. "I don't know, fisherman. I haven't thought of one yet."

"Well, nigger, you'd better start thinkin' of one and damned fast, 'fore we get our asses all shot to Hell."

Walker looked away from Jackson. He felt a bone-numbing weariness suddenly creep over him.

"Hey, man, I'm talkin' to you!"

"I heard ya, fisherman," Walker growled, turning his head sideways. "You'll be the first to know when I come up with somethin'.'"

There was no plan, he knew. Just set the warbird down somewhere, move in, and let it rip.

Walker squished out a mouthful of blood. He was ready to kill something. Anything.

Killing. Lots of it.

He would make it justify his own dead end.

His own road to Hell.

When he saw the main Fourth Reich garrison, Leroy Walker knew they had a problem.

And he suspected they'd bitten off a little more than they could chew. With or without the white dudes.

Jackson suspected as much, too. And the fisherman let Walker know about his dismay. "Now what? You're the big nigger on the block. Now what?"

"Turn it around!" Walker snarled at the pilot.

The pilot ignored Walker. The big ex-heavyweight smashed the butt of his Atchisson off the pilot's helmet.

"I said turn it away, motherfucker! Now. You head downriver and set us down."

Barnes, standing beside Walker, surveyed the compound that sprawled along the Congo River and into the valley with a grim expression. "Look at that, man," he breathed, damn near awestruck.

Yeah, Walker looked, all right. As the chopper pilot banked to the west, he took in the massive Nazi operation. He counted maybe twenty helicopter gunships along the shores of the Congo River. Big warbirds with the same firepower-equipped dimensions as their Spectre. And that wasn't counting another dozen flying battleships on the compound grounds. A death fleet. A Fourth Reich *Luftwaffe*.

At the moment, transport trucks were rolling away from the hills. Rows of black drums lined the foothills of the abandoned, dried-up mines. Containers were being loaded onto the gunships.

"What's in those containers?" Walker asked the pilot.

The pilot turned his head slightly. Just beneath his dark-tinted visor, his lips stretched in a cold smile. "Nerve gas."

"Where's it going?" Barnes demanded.

"Just about anywhere and everywhere. You are American, *ja?*" The pilot chuckled.

"What the hell's that mean?" Walker growled.

"The U.S. Army has recently developed a new 155mm nuclear projectile. It has replaced the old eight-inch projectile. It does not require field assembly or a special spotting round." The pilot laughed again. "Only setting and insertion of an electronic fuse. Of course, I don't expect any of you to understand this. But it is enough to say that our men have modified the warhead to be fired from the rocket pods mounted on the gunships."

Barnes and Walker looked at each other. Jackson breathed a curse.

"We have four such warheads now." The pilot laughed. "Four more are being assembled to go to South Africa. Immediately."

"They're going to nuke the homelands," Barnes rasped, a dark, concerned look filling his eyes as he turned away from the pilot.

"No," the pilot corrected. "Kinshasa first. The government of Zaire believes Schnell will be coming to pay it off with the Nazi gold it had been promised upon completion of our work here. Yes. Mobutu and his black baboons," the pilot sneered, "will be paid off. In thermonuclear spades."

"You'd murder millions of people," Walker growled. "For what?"

The pilot turned and looked at Walker as if he were speaking to an idiot. "For the salvation of this continent. The blacks here all believe they should be granted independence. That might be fine if the white man did not come here and create and develop the economy of any country in Africa worth mentioning. And, I will add, that might be fine if the blacks could even govern themselves."

Walker felt his rage building toward a murderous explosion. "Maybe if you 'superior' Afrikaaners treated the blacks here like they were something other than animals; maybe if you granted them some self-respect, you might find that the black man is quite capable of governing himself. Every bit as capable as Whitey."

"*Ach.* Listen, my friend, if this country was turned over tomorrow to the blacks, there would mass tribal warfare. There would be a slaughter that you could not even begin to imagine. Ignorance, you stupid bastard, is why the black African, for the most part, is still up in the trees. And the ones who have been brought out of the Dark Ages owe it to the white man. If it wasn't for the white man here, Africa would have already fallen into the hands of the Soviets. And, I must add, free Africa is in danger of doing that now. Particularly if the proapartheid revolutionaries have their way. It amazes the Afrikaaners how you self-righteous, moralizing Americans are always telling the rest of the world how to run their countries. When you cannot even control your own affairs. Just stop for a moment and take a look at your black inner-city slums. Are they really any different from the home-lands in South Africa? And what about your Indian reservations? What about the land the Indian was forced off of? No, your politicians and masses see only what they want to see. Or are told to see by your spineless, self-glorifying media."

Barnes whistled. "Man, with an attitude like that, I ain't even gonna bother."

Yeah, Walker knew there was only one way he was going to change this Fourth Reich bigot's mind.

"One thing's for sure, brother," he said to Barnes. "We've gotta stop those gunships from getting off the ground."

The pilot laughed, long and hard. "The three of you? Against maybe three hundred fully trained commandos?"

"Keep laughing, asshole," Walker warned.

"Three hundred?" Jackson echoed. "Like I said before, man, now what?"

"Look, fisherman," Barnes rasped. "You ain't got the balls for this, you can sit tight. We're going in. I ain't gonna sit around and worry about getting my ass blown off by a bunch of Nazis that would nuke or gas half of black Africa. You put these guys into power in Pretoria, you think things'll get any better for the blacks here? Fuck it. I'll die if I have to, to stop those gunships from taking off."

Walker found himself agreeing with Barnes in the worst way. No, he thought, suddenly longing for yesteryear, he wasn't going to make the cover of *Ring* magazine for this. But maybe, just maybe, there was a real reason why he had fucked up so bad in life. One thing was for damned sure, he thought. There was a reason for him being there now.

"Drop it down here," he said, looking at the wide strip of muddy shoreline below.

The pilot dropped the gunship down on the shoreline, landing skids sinking into the thick mud.

Walker looked at the pilot. The guy just sat there smiling at him defiantly, hatefully.

"Thanks for the ride," the ex-heavyweight said, lifting the Atchisson. "Give my regards to Hitler and Himmler in the big H."

The Atchisson roared on full-auto. Walker held the trigger back, the big twelve-bore shotgun bucking in his massive fists. Deafening peals bounced around in the cockpit and fuselage. Behind Walker, Jackson recoiled in horror as the pilot's head and torso blew apart. Walker unleashed the whole goddamn twenty-round magazine, exploding shells sizzling fifty number-two and double-ought steel balls, dismembering the pilot's arms as if they were torn off by invisible meat cleavers. Sparks showered from the erupting instrument panel. Blood, gore, and bits of organs splattered the panel and glass bubble. Hurricaning rounds blasted out the window of the cockpit door. When the Atchisson pounded out its last round, there was nothing left of the neo-Nazi pilot above the waist. Nothing.

"Jesus God," Jackson breathed.

"Let's go," Walker said, tight-lipped, ejecting the empty magazine.

As they disembarked the gunship, boots squishing down into the soft mud, Walker plucked an M15 off his webbing and pulled the pin. He tossed the grenade, underhanded, into the fuselage. Quickly, the three black Death Row soldiers ran away from the chopper. Seconds later, a slick, roiling thermite blast ripped through the bowels of the gunship, pulverizing the Nazi warbird. Twisted wreckage blew out over the river.

"Burn, bitch, burn," Walker muttered, giving the fiery debris a final look.

Jackson appeared shaken by what he'd seen moments ago. But he said nothing, following Barnes and Walker into the maw of the jungle.

Into the law of the jungle.

A gleaming heap of gold, diamonds, and other gems were piled in a small clearing near the outpost ruins, where Hangman and his three white warriors stood, drawing contentedly on cigarettes.

Williams cast the confiscated treasure a long, rueful stare. "Hey, Sarge, look."

"Yeah, I'm looking," he said, a disgusted edge to his voice. "You've got to learn to let go of the world, all of you. Leave it behind you. Someday you'll be checking out. Maybe sooner than you think," he added.

None of them had gotten the message, Hangman sensed. Death, they believed—and with plenty of damned justification—awaited them at the end of this operation's rope. Forget all that bullshit about not being afraid to die, the Hangman thought. Some guys had a knack for lying to themselves about dying. The Hangman knew that a warrior fought more fiercely to hold onto life when the final hour dawned. And his barbarians would fight until the last bitter second. Even against him. Especially against him.

"The Israelis just left about fifteen minutes ago, Cap'n. Headed up the tracks. They said the main Nazi garrison is about twenty klicks northeast, along the river."

"Let's move out. Double time."

"What about your soul-brother buddies?" White wanted to know.

"What about them?"

"Well, hell, don't you think they'll be a little pissed off if you leave 'em out of this?"

"You care?"

White seemed to think about that for a moment. "Should I?" he growled defensively.

"Off your asses. Time's wasting. This thing won't end here. Believe me, everybody's going to get a piece of the action. Probably more than any of you want."

With that, the Hangman led his cutthroats away from that kill-zone. As he ran after the departed West German–Israeli commando squad, he had some time to think, though he kept a wary eye on his troops.

Africa, from Tripoli to Cape Town, was a mess. A frightening mess. Violent overthrow of the white government in South Africa would do nobody a shred of good. Apartheid sure wasn't the answer, either. Mass genocide was the twisted ambition of men living in fear and hatred. And Communism would mean a living hell for everybody, inside and outside of Africa.

Reforms, yeah. Justice, yeah. But where the hell was that, anywhere in the world? It was a hell of a thing when good men could only bring about justice through the barrel of a gun. But here they were, prepared to save perhaps an entire continent by having to slaughter anything that now opposed them.

"Up ahead, Cap'n."

White's sharp voice jarred the Hangman back to the present. Fifty meters ahead, the SOD man spotted the Nazi-hunting force.

Troops guarding the commando unit's flanks alerted the brothers Husseini to the approach of the Americans.

"You're late," Ruben Husseini growled at the Hangman as he led his troops to the front.

"I know," the Hangman dryly remarked. "I had to

lecture one of my guys on loyalty, love, and compassion for his fellow man."

A scowl hinted at Ruben Husseini's features.

"You got some kind of plan?" the Hangman wanted to know "Or are we just going to be in the way?"

"The plan, my American friend," the elder Husseini said, "is to go in and annihilate the compound. We kill anything and everything that moves. We continue to do the same until the Nazi scourge is ended here."

Mac White, Pygmy arrow still stuck in the crown of the commando hat perched on his head, looked at the Hangman and said, "God, I love that kinda talk."

CHAPTER TWELVE

The shipment was late. Hours overdue. And they had not been able to make radio contact with the train checkpoint.

Alois Schnell was worried. Something was very wrong. Very wrong indeed.

At the moment, the SS *Reichsführer* watched as his Boer and German dissident forces prepared the attack. SS *Reichsführer, ja*, he thought. Decked out in his SS uniform, there was no "former" in Schnell's mind. There was no "ex-SS."

Yesteryear was not dead.

If only there were more German blood here. Ruefully, Schnell shook his head. A hand full of Dutchmen and a smattering of Brits. It was a shame, he thought. The German fury was going to march again, but the lineage had been bastardized. Just how much did this bastardized Fourth Reich now believe in their mission, he had to wonder.

He would soon find out.

The hour of truth had arrived.

He saw his brother striding across the grounds, coming toward him in his own SS uniform. Proud, *ja,* he should have been. But proud he wasn't. There was something troubling Herbert, he sensed. Doubt? Regret? Sorrow?

It didn't matter, he told himself. Several of the gunships were ready to fly out. Two of them armed with the warheads and loaded down with nerve gas were destined for Leopoldville. The government of Zaire was expecting its final payoff.

The Zairians had no idea that the German fury was coming to claim their useless, needless existence, he thought. The government of Zaire, in their own vested interests, had cooperated with the Fourth Reich. The blacks believed they were going to be part of the new German conquest. There was nothing so pleasurable as handing the naive their just reward, Schnell knew.

Still, the Republic of South Africa would not be an easy conquest.

But the South African dissidents and their leaders had amassed near the Botswana border. The assassination squads were at this very moment prepared to begin the revolution. The climate was right. The road to a violent overthrow, to a *coup d'état,* had long since been paved by both the pro- and antiapartheid forces.

Pretoria, Schnell envisioned, would feel the terrible wrath of his own *Wehrmacht blitzkrieg.* As Yugoslavia and Greece had felt the fury of the Third Reich. His own gunship *Luftwaffe* would lay waste to any resistance as soon as more white South African dissidents sided with his new Reich.

Schnell resolved himself to not fall victim to his own ego once he captured Pretoria. There would be serious problems to be dealt with immediately. There would be resistance.

America would be a serious resistance problem. But, Schnell thought, there was some movement going through that country now and it was growing daily. What was it called? The Order, the Silent Brotherhood. *Ja,* that was it. *Scheisskopfs,* he thought. They were claiming to be the true chosen people. They were claiming thick European blood. *What a disgrace. What a joke.* They were nothing but ignorant, inarticulate, inferior... "crackers," he believed they were called. A band of unworthy white misfits violently sworn to overthrow the United States government, something they called the Zionist Occupation government. When the time came, though, Schnell knew they could be used. He would prey on their minds, their fears, and their basic sense of inferiority. When they had served their usefulness to him and to the Reich, he would then have them lick the assholes of the Jews and permit captured blacks to kill them painfully, brutally, disgracefully.

"Alois?"

He looked at his younger brother. There was concern on Herbert's face. It troubled Alois Schnell.

"Are you not worried about the shipment? Perhaps Kinshasa has decided to move against us?"

"Nein," Alois Schnell scoffed. "They would do nothing so foolish, believe me, my brother. They have nothing to gain by such recklessness. And everything to lose if they conspire against us. I have offered them the Transvaal, which I promised to annex once we come into power. Of course, the government of Zaire will not be around to witness our victory."

The anxiety did not fade from Herbert Schnell's eyes. "I feel we should send out a reconnaissance team to search for that train, brother. Our American suppliers have been murdered by an unknown assailant. Perhaps even the CIA is onto us, do you think?"

Alois Schnell thought about that for a moment. He nodded, looked around the compound. Rotor blades began to spin on several of the warbirds.

"Perhaps you are right, brother. I am worried

about the shipment, also. I will dispatch an air-and-ground recon team immediately." He searched the dense jungle foliage to the south. He looked up at the cloudless blue sky, the sun a blazing yellow fireball directly overhead. "There is a stillness today ...something in the air I do not trust. I do not like this feeling of foreboding that I have."

Alois Schnell looked at his brother. Yes, something, he decided, was very wrong with Herbert. His younger brother suddenly appeared very old and very tired.

And filled with doubt.

They discussed the final assault plan as they cut a tortuous path through the jungle.

The Hangman liked it. And he liked the way the brothers Husseini thought. But then again, the Israelis and the West Germans were head-and-shoulders above anyone else when it came to guerilla warfare and antiterrorist fighting. These guys were search and destroy, take no prisoners, all the way. No political bullshit here. And, yeah, after seeing what they had done to the Nazis at the Fourth Reich checkpoint station, he would tip his commando hat to these guys in respect any day. Hell, he might even buy the first couple of rounds.

"Then, it is agreed, my American friend," Ruben Husseini said to the Hangman, "that we surround the main garrison and destroy it in a *blitzkrieg?*"

"You got that right," Hangman said, following the Husseinis up the winding path. "We have to keep in mind, though, that there might be some hostages at the compound."

In silence, three columns of soldiers forged ahead through the jungle. Vines and brush tore at faces and clothes. Leeches clung to bare skin. It was a slow, tough, agonizing trek. But everyone moved with a relentless indifference to the steamy, stinking air, the cuts inflicted by thorny brush, and the writhing, sucking leeches. Not even his own soldiers, the Hangman noticed, bitched now. They had turned deadly serious. Yeah, they were ready.

Ruben Husseini nodded. "I agree. The loss of any hostages would indeed blacken our mission. You have my word that we will do everything in our power to see that those hostages are unharmed. But, I am sure you understand the grave consequences if we fail to annihilate the Fourth Reich. Hostages and slave workers will have to be dealt with, I am afraid, during the heat of the battle. Some may die," he said, hacking away a tangled nest of vines with his machete, "when the Nazis realize that their Judgment Day is upon them. I do not mean to sound callous, but the success of our mission here outweighs a few lives."

Unfortunately, the SOD man found himself agreeing with the brothers Husseini on the hostage matter. The only thing that could save all of the hostages was a quick and totally annihilating strike against the enemy. With their backs pressed to the wall, he knew the enemy might just start putting bullets through people's heads.

Hangman guessed they were now five kilometers from the garrison. He had already radioed Spectre and given the gunship's navigator coordinates and instructions. The pilot was to set down along the shore of the Congo River, strategically placing himself five kilometers from the garrison. There, he was to await further orders. Air-fire support, Hangman knew, would be used. But he would wait to bring Spectre in, opting to recon the garrison to get a feel for the numbers first. There was no point in showing his ace in the hole to the Nazis too soon. And air-fire support was something the Husseinis agreed to, also. Simply because they had none. The Nazi-hunters, he learned, had been dropped off across the river in a savanna early that morning. They had then manned large inflatable rafts across the river. Their fixed-wing gunship, he had been told, was returning just after dawn tomorrow. It would pick them up at that time. If they weren't at the recovery site, it was to be assumed they had failed or were dead.

That brought the Husseinis to another point.

"If the trail of the Fourth Reich leads to South Africa," Abraham Husseini said, "you, my friend, and your commandos will be on your own. Mossad clearly warned us against any venture into South Africa. Intelligence believes that the heart of the Nazi monster is here. Any other guilty parties, whether in Mobutu's government or in South Africa, will be brought to justice through other means."

"That is, as far as we are concerned," Ruben was quick to point out. "As far as you are concerned, you may do whatever you wish after we have eliminated all targets here. We pull out of here tomorrow morning. No matter what."

"If there are guilty parties in Zaire or South Africa," Abraham Husseini said, "it might be best if they were uncovered. Alive. If the scheme to overthrow South Africa were made world knowledge, perhaps the proapartheid forces may seriously reconsider their position. Justice may show the Afrikaaners the ugliness of their apartheid policy. Indeed, internal destruction of the Republic of South Africa is in the worst interest for both our countries. Violent overthrow of that country would devastate everyone, except the Soviets, of course. South Africa, the most technologically advanced, most economically powerful country in Africa, is a prize worth capturing for Russia. If the Afrikaaners cannot create a more stable internal situation, then I am afraid the Soviet cancer will spread and consume the Republic. The apartheid mess in South Africa is a situation they are most certainly exploiting. Unfortunately, the black man has always believed that the Soviets have come to liberate them from their white oppressors. The situation in Zimbabwe is a perfect and frightening example of how effectively the Soviets can deceive. And just how much worse is a black man's life under Communist tyranny.

"Our country is allied with South Africa, and we intend to keep that alliance. Both of our countries daily face the threat of military strikes by an enemy that has us completely surrounded. We must adopt a certain stance and abide by that stance, no matter what the rest of the world thinks. Still, the Republic's apartheid policy is unsettling to us. As you know, we are not that far removed, my friend, from a very similar situation. The genesis of another holocaust has obviously already begun."

The warbird came out of nowhere.

Before any of the commandos had time to react, miniguns were blazing, churning the jungle canopy to shreds. A veil of fire roared through the foliage. Door gunners manned M60s, the mounted machine guns blazing lead behind the streaming hell-storm of 7.62mm flesh-shredders.

Instantly, the Hangman, his Death Row soldiers, and the Nazi-hunters took cover. Without hesitation, several commandos triggered LAW 80s. Rocket-propelled HEAT rounds sizzled through the shredded canopy. A trio of warheads pulped the giant gunship. Rolling fireballs thundered, boiled over the tree line.

"They came from the south," Hangman told the Husseinis.

"That means they've seen the outpost," Ruben Husseini said.

"Or what's left of it," Hangman said. "I'm sure they radioed their reconnaissance ahead to the main garrison. Looks like our surprise *blitzkrieg* was a good idea in the planning stage, fellas."

"Let's move it out!" Husseini ordered his men.

As the Nazi-hunters split up their numbers to cover the rear and flanks, Hangman reached for his radio handset. Time to put his ace in the hole on emergency standby.

"What's the plan, Cap'n?" Mac White wanted to know.

"Still the same," he told the ex-Klansman as flaming wreckage crashed through the jungle canopy behind him. "I'm just getting a little extra firepower ready. Annihilation from above. And I know you love that kind of talk, 'cause you're people-lovin' kind of guys."

Mac White gave the Hangman a thumbs-up. "You know it, Cap'n."

CHAPTER THIRTEEN

The combined American–Israeli–West German strike force moved in on the Fourth Reich garrison. One squad each of the Husseinis' commandos parted from the flanks to take the assault in from the east and west fringes of the hill-and-tree-surrounded compound. A straightforward scissors-type attack. Move in, open fire, mop up.

The Hangman liked it, and he hadn't even fired his first shot. Already the SOD man felt as if he were six inches off the ground from an adrenaline rush. But there were always problems, he knew, even with the best-laid plans.

Striking the garrison in broad daylight would mean casualties, the Hangman thought. Plenty of casualties. But after the fateful encounter with the Nazi warbird, waiting became an impossibility.

Then, the watchtower guards spotted the advance of the Star of David forces and alerted the compound.

The sudden wail of the siren atop the command

post put an instant damper on any *blitzkrieg* tactics. Brown-and-black-uniformed troops instantly scrambled to take cover behind transport trucks or sandbag piles. Some made it. Some died during the initial strike.

Ruben Husseini cursed and signaled to launch the attack.

LAW 80s belched deadly payloads from the jungle brush. Dozens of Uzis cut loose, hailing 9mm lead over Nazis who had not reached cover quickly enough.

A HEAT round streaked across the compound and vaporized the watchtower, hurtling shredded Nazi remains skyward.

As roiling fireclouds dismembered scurrying Nazis and pulverized transport trucks and Land Rovers near the command post, the Hangman led his Death Row three into the heat of the firefight. Head-on into the fires of Hell.

Mac White wasted no time fucking around. The MM-1 coughed repeatedly in the ex-Klansman's hands, HE projectiles rocketing into the chaos as he picked anything that even resembled a target. Six consecutive explosions vomited the command post and the troop bivouacs from the valley floor. Within seconds, the compound became a flaming hellground.

Helicopter gunships began to lift off.

The ex-Klansman turned his hard-eyed attention toward the warbirds with their genocide payload. A Rebel yell ripping from his throat, White triggered two HE rounds. And two gunships became blazing, misshapen hulls. Showering wreckage quickly pounded into gunships preparing to lift off. A horrible screeching of metal followed as rotor blades intercepted the debris. Choppers collided like battling sword-wielding giants, erupting into mountainous walls of fire. Auxiliary fuel tanks blew, spraying fiery waves over scattering enemy numbers, torching Nazis. A flaming, out-of-control warbird slammed into a huge fuel tank, sending a volcanic eruption of fire whooshing skyward.

The Hangman had expected a big operation, yeah. But he hadn't expected to find a mini-*Luftwaffe*. This place had to be razed.

Moments later, a trio of warbirds loomed above the tree line near the airstrip, rocket pods belching flame and smoke.

Death found the Star of David.

Explosions ripped through the heart of the Israeli–West German left flank, launching bodies on tongues of geysering fire. Rocket teams instantly sacrificed themselves to bring those warbirds down with HEAT rounds. As the trio of deathbirds were blown out of the sky by the LAWs, those Star of David rocket teams were drilled into the ground by a relentless 5.56mm lead hurricane from Nazi R-4s.

But those Nazis became targets, dancing death jigs as the Hangman burned hot lead over their positions, his flaming Uzi muzzle parting the wall of fire in front of him. As White took out more Nazi cover with HE rounds, the Hangman surged forward. Williams and Schnell covered the SOD man's flanks. Running side by side, the one-eyed pirate and the German merc pulped any enemy numbers with a combined Uzi and SPAS-12 roar. It was hit, bolt forward, secure cover. Kill, run, cover.

Hangman saw brown-uniformed soldiers manning two antiaircraft guns atop the hill. German 88s. Big firepower, he knew. Afrika Korps firepower. The kind of firepower that had to be taken out right away.

"The cannons!" he yelled at White, dropping to a knee behind the flaming ruins of a transport truck. "Take out the fucking cannons!"

"I'm out of rounds!" White yelled back, fumbling to get his rucksack off. "Gimme a goddamn second!"

"Give him a hand, somebody, goddamnit!" Hangman yelled as more HEAT rounds shook the earth around them, lethal debris whistling overhead, spearing the earth with razor-sharp wreckage.

For somebody wearing the Star of David, it was a little too late again.

The German 88s began to shell the jungle. A dozen soldiers of the Star of David were shredded by the concussive blasts. More Israeli–West German commandos, surging toward the compound from the flanks, corkscrewed to the ground as R-4s and FN-LARs barked from the northern hills. Cover fire was instantly provided for the gunships. Somebody, the SOD man knew, wanted those warbirds to fly the hell out of there in one piece.

Hangman spotted two guys halfway up the hill, directly above the mouth of a cave, with HK G-11 Caseless Assault Rifles. And they were doing a hell of a job covering for the warbirds, too. The G-11, Hangman knew, could spit out an incredible two thousand rounds per minute. Three-round bursts could be fired within ninety milliseconds, and its 4.7mm slug could pierce a steel helmet from more than five hundred meters out. And the guys with the G-11s weren't dicking around, either. If the Hangman and his troops didn't get their act together in a heartbeat, they could count themselves out.

Down, yeah, but not out yet.

And the G-11 gunners were finding flesh with lightning, raking flashes over the charging Husseini force.

As the Hangman and Schnell covered, Williams handed White the HE rounds for the MM-1. Suddenly, lead started chewing up the ground behind White. Whirling, Hangman saw a Nazi gunship soaring toward them. Miniguns opened up on them, a line of blazing fire tracking their cover.

They were dead shit!

Then the black warbird erupted directly over their heads. Twisted, flaming wreckage hammered to the ground around the Hangman and his troops.

"Hey, Cap'n! Look at these guys!"

Turning, the Hangman saw Walker, Barnes, and Jackson running toward them.

Walker, MM-1 smoking in his hands, growled, "Don't you fuckers know how to say *danke schön?*"

"How the hell did you dudes get here?" Williams yelled.

White glanced at the battered faces of Walker and Barnes. "Who lit into you two?"

Hangman briefly wondered that, too. Now wasn't the time for any reunion or twenty questions, though. Now was the time to get his war machine on a rampaging roll.

Walker turned instant combat attention to the German 88 crews. Dropping to a knee, the ex-heavyweight unleashed the MM-1. White joined Walker a second later in the burial of the heavier Nazi firepower. A flaming crater became the headstone for the antiaircraft crews.

The bulk of the *Luftwaffe* forces ascended above the jungle tree line. Heading out with their mass-murder payloads. Two of the black warbirds flashed into fiery thunderclouds as LAW 80 HEAT rounds zeroed in on the gunships.

Moments later, the gunship with the skull and crossbones soared over the tree line to the south.

Williams pointed at Spectre and shouted, "Hey, Sarge!"

Hangman saw their gunship as it streaked over the compound. He pointed to the radio handset and crooked a graveyard grin. "I left it on."

White let out a Rebel yell at the sight of Spectre. "Yeah, babeeee! The boys in the fucking band are back! Play me some butt-kicking blues! *Deutschland über fucking Alleeeeees!*" he screamed, shredding a half-dozen Nazis fleeing for the mouth of a cave with an earthquaking warhead.

Walker and Jackson guarded the kill-team's flanks. The ex-heavyweight's MM-1 took out a huge radar dish, then flipped a deuce-and-a-half up into the air. Hitlerians tumbled from the flaming wreck as the transport truck crushed down on its side. Screams shrilled the air when Nazis were pinned beneath the warped hull, fire consuming their faces and flailing arms.

White concentrated a three-round HE burst on the G-11 gunners. Roaring fireballs hurled them off the craggy hillside, bloody, dismembered rags that splattered the dry, dusty earth.

Rockets whooshed away from Spectre's mounted pods. Two Nazi warbirds boiled into rolling clouds of fire over the jungle tree line.

Hangman saw the remaining Fourth Reich force retreating into the caves. The specialist, Williams, Jackson, and Barnes hosed fleeing Hitlerians with an Uzi fusillade. Even Schnell unslung his Uzi, cutting down a half-dozen Nazis as they descended the hill. Dead men flopped down on top of Hitlerians scrambling for retreat. Bodies crunched, spun, thudded into each other as 9mm hell-storms churned up brown uniforms.

Hangman slapped a fresh thirty-two-round clip home. He grabbed his radio headset. "Stick around, fly-boy!" he ordered the pilot. "We're going into the mine, and we might need air cover coming out if those gunships decide to fly back."

"I've got seven warbirds heading for the horizon," the pilot declared.

"Forget 'em, for now. That's an order. Over."

"A couple of those warbirds got nuclear projectiles on them, man!" Walker told the specialist.

Hangman looked at Walker.

Walker quickly summed up their fight at the village, then the flight and their captive pilot's story.

"Odds are if there were only two," Hangman said, "those seven weren't it."

"You hope."

Yeah, he hoped, all right. He radioed Spectre's pilot. "Dragonship, come in."

"Dragonship here. Over."

"Follow those warbirds, fly-boy. Keep a fix on them. I want you back here in fifteen minutes, though. We're pulling out and going after them. Copy?"

"Loud and clear. Over."

"Move it out!" Hangman ordered his troops.

Spreading out in a staggered formation, the Hangman led his war machine toward the caves. Nazis provided cover from the mouth of two caves as their comrades retreated deeper into the mines. The remaining gunships of the *Luftwaffe* were now being seized by Star of David commandos storming the airstrip. Relentless Uzi fire shredded Nazis, kicking them back into the fuselages of their warbirds.

To his right flank, the Hangman saw the brothers Husseini charging the caves. Star of David commandos bolted from the cover of flaming wreckage, Uzis barking.

"Frag 'em!" Hangman ordered his troops, plucking an MK2 off his webbing, pulling the pin out with his teeth.

"Deutschland über Alles!" the SOD man heard Mac White scream as seven minibombs hurtled toward the wide cave maws. Hell, if he didn't know better, he would have sworn he just glimpsed regret in White's eyes. *But, hell, they were killing the supreme trumpeters of Caucasian supremacy, weren't they?*

Frag bombs exploded just in front of the caves. Shrapnel mixed with white phosphorus from somebody's M15. Hellish shrieks ripped from the caves. Chunks of sheared-off rubble exploded away from the maw. Human torches stumbled from the swirling smoke, slapping at heads and faces.

"Burn, bitch, burn!" Walker shouted, strapping the MM-1 around his shoulder and then unslinging the Atchisson.

The chatter of SMG fire and the screams of dying demons in his ears, the Hangman led the surge to the caves. Slugs suddenly stitched the ground in front. He looked up, glimpsed the two Hitlerians near the top of the hill. Their HK91s flew from their hands as Barnes and Williams gutted them open with 9mm Parabellum hell-riders.

The Nazi demons flailing about on the ground, the stench of burning flesh tearing into his nose, the Hangman threw himself up against the wall of rock, his troops flanking the maw of the cave. Lead whined off the stone above their heads and the rubble piled in the opening as pencils of flame parted the darkness down the cave.

At the next maw down from the Hangman, the brothers Husseini, backed by the LAW 80 fire that whooshed down the tunnel, led the charge into the mine.

As enemy fire peppered their position, Hangman, Williams, and Barnes lobbed MK2s down the tunnel. Seconds later, saffron flashes produced screams of agony. Cordite, blood, smoke choking into his nose and lungs, the Hangman raced down the tunnel, jumping over twisted, crimson rugmats of Nazi flesh. Jackson and White trailed the charge, covering the team's rear. The bark of automatic weapons and SMG fire sounded ahead, rolling thunder that bounced off the walls of the tunnel around the Hangman and his Killsquad.

At the end of the tunnel, the Hangman flung himself up against the wall. He took in the underground complex quickly. Enemy numbers were running down gangways, heading for the holes along the far wall. Beneath the metal planks stretched a sea of black drums.

The force of the brothers Husseini moved onto the gangway. Hangman and his troops, kneeling in the tunnel, opened up with Uzi fire. Waves of sizzling lead washed over the retreating Nazi numbers. Bullets ricocheted off metal. Bodies flipped over guardrails, plunging for the sea of drums. Expending clips, the Hangman and his soldiers rammed home fresh mags and continued in the bloody burial of the Fourth Reichers. The roaring blast of SMG fire became total, deafening within seconds, the craggy walls of the underground complex trapping the hellish chatter along with the screams of the mortally wounded.

When the enemy numbers were finally decimated and the stragglers and the wounded made one final desperate run for the far tunnels, the Hangman turned to check his troops.

"Anybody hit?" he asked.

Then they all noticed something.

One of them was unaccounted for.

"Hey," Williams rasped. "Where's the German?"

"Anybody see him come in with us?" Hangman asked.

"He was right beside me when we hit the caves, Cap'n."

Walker scowled and looked the Hangman dead in the eye. "Looks like the German chose sides."

The Hangman muttered a curse under his breath. Something told him that, yeah, Walker was right.

Schnell was now walking among the damned.

CHAPTER FOURTEEN

Lucien Schnell had to keep reminding himself, *These are not the same Teutonic people that had taken country after country after country.... These are not the same Teutonic people who had arisen from the ashes the Jews and the Allies had heaped on them after World War I.... These are not the same Teutonic people who had stormed into Greece, the same day as their blitzkrieg on Yugoslavia, kicked the fucking scheiss out of the British Empire Army, then hung a swastika from the Acropolis and said, "We are here. And you had better learn to like it. Or your miserable, conquered ass is fried." Nein. These are not the same superior Teutonic warriors who had come within a hair of conquering the entire planet.*

This was not the German fury.

This was the rabble left over from a dead dream.

If Lucien Schnell did not tell himself that, he could not have pulled the trigger of his Uzi. But he did. At the end of the tunnel, he saw perhaps seven

133

brown-uniformed Nazis scythed down on the sizzling end of his Parabellum stream.

During the confusion of the battle, he had left the *Amerikaners*. This was not their war, he thought. Nor was this the Jews' war.

This, he told himself, was his war.

He was the only German fury there.

He was the only one who could vindicate the Teutonic people. He was the only one who could erase the horror of the past forever from his mind.

Indeed, he hoped the *Amerikaners* were dead.

Indeed, the Jewish commandos deserved death, too.

After slapping a fresh thirty-two-round clip into his Uzi, he strapped the Israeli SMG around his shoulder. Then, his favored autoshotgun filled his hands.

Swiftly, the German merc moved out of the tunnel. Stepping onto the metal gangway, he looked right. A good hundred yards away, he saw the combined *Amerikaner–Jew* forces as they poured into the underground complex.

Then Schnell spotted something else.

And time stood still for the German mercenary.

A man dressed in an SS uniform ran down the opposite gangway. The SS man stopped for a moment beneath the huge swastika banner hanging from the ceiling. Schnell made eye contact with the man.

And there was no mistaking who that SS officer was.

His father.

Alois Schnell.

The Surgeon.

The Butcher of Auschwitz.

A camp *doktor.*

A monster.

Slowly, as if he were moving through his own dream, Lucien Schnell stepped across the gangway. His gaze stayed locked on his father.

Alois Schnell's jaw went slack. His eyes widened.

As his father moved toward the tunnel, Schnell rasped, "*Halten Sie! Stop!*"

Alois Schnell stumbled over a rock, hitting the gangway on his stomach. Looking up moments later, he found the tall, blue-eyed, stone-faced warrior looming over him. He couldn't believe his eyes. He was looking at a mirror image of himself twenty, maybe thirty years ago.

Alois Schnell climbed to his feet and braced himself against the rock wall. His lips trembled. "Lucien?"

The German merc swung away from his father suddenly, stepping into the mouth of the tunnel as if guarding against any possible escape.

The Surgeon took a step toward his son.

Schnell lifted the SPAS, aiming the snout with unwavering menace at his father's chest. "*Nein.*"

The German merc stared at his father's gaunt, heavily lined features. He saw pride, arrogance, fear in those deep-set blue eyes. But he wasn't exactly sure what he saw on his father's face. And he wasn't sure exactly what he felt, now that he had reached the end of his own tortured destiny.

Questions buzzed angrily through Lucien Schnell's head. He heard a jumbled maze of distorted sound. His voice in his ears. The roar of SMG fire in the distance. Shouts. Screams. Curses.

Finally the German merc felt his lips part. And all he could say was, "Why?"

Alois Schnell barked out a strange-sounding nervous laugh. "Why?" he echoed. "Son, my son . . . you have to ask me why?"

Bitter rage filled Lucien Schnell. "*Ja.* I am asking you now. Why? Why have I been forced to live with his thing on my head since I was a boy? Where were you when my mother died? When she told me the truth? Where were you?" he hissed, suddenly recalling the look of horror and shame in his mother's eyes when she told him about his father and uncle, the Surgeons, in her moment of death. "Why? Why, then, did you run like some dog?"

Anger flashed through Alois Schnell's eyes. He drew a breath, squared his shoulders. The unrelenting, maniacal pride of the German fury held strong.

"You cannot begin to understand, Lucien. You were not there when our country was reduced to rubble by our enemies. You did not see how our great country was handed over to the Jewish pagans. No, my son, I cannot even expect you to begin to understand the why."

No, he did not understand. Any of it. Lucien Schnell only understood his own grief, the years of unceasing torment, the memories that had haunted his every move across the world. In search of his father and uncle. In search of what, he asked himself.

In search of death was his only answer. *Ja*, indirectly he blamed the killings of those ten young girls on this man who stood before him, proud, unforgiving.

And unforgivable.

The SPAS became a leaden weight in his grasp. He began to lower it by his side.

"Schnell! Schnell!"

He heard the pounding of bootsteps on the gangway, saw the *Amerikaners* in the blurry corner of his eye, where a wetness began to burn into his vision.

"Son, you do not understand. Accept it. We can leave this place. Together. Now, Lucien! Before it is too late."

This was not his father, he heard his mind say. This was a monster. But if this man was such a monster, then what was he? *What was he?* What?

And, no, it wasn't he who was going to do it, as he lifted the SPAS in his hands.

"Son, no. No! You do not understand."

"Nein," Schnell heard a distant voice in his ears say, unaware that it was his own voice, but knowing

that it was not he who was about to do justice to the damned of the past. To the damned in the present.

It was the past, he knew, that was going to do it.

"I...cannot understand," Lucien Schnell said.

"Son! Noooo!"

The German merc leveled the SPAS on his father's chest. Closing his eyes, he squeezed the trigger. The peal of the lethal retort rolled around in his head, shattering his senses. Why? A voice called from the darkness of his mind. *Why did it have to be him?*

Slowly, he forced his eyes open. He saw his father outstretched below him, draped over the black drums. Blood gushed from the gaping, ragged hole in his father's chest. Out of the corner of his eye, he glimpsed the green-eyed CIA bastard and the other *Amerikaners* running across the gangway toward him. For a second, he felt compelled to turn the SPAS on them. He could take them all out, he knew. So easy. So fitting. So damned justified.

He could have ended it there.

But for some reason he didn't.

"I saw the guy close his eyes when he shot the old man, Sarge."

"Shut up."

Schnell looked down at the thing he had shot. Alois Schnell's mouth opened. "There is...no German...blood...here....It is...not...our...defeat."

"You going to be all right, Schnell?"

The Surgeon's head lolled to the side. He twitched once, then was utterly still.

The SPAS lowered by Schnell's side. He felt empty, drained. His father's final words rattled around inside his head.

And, yes, he wanted to believe those words.

Leroy Walker kicked the wooden door off its hinges. Atchisson sweeping up by his side, he surged off the gangway into the room.

And froze in the doorway.

Suddenly, Leroy Walker felt like some prisoner caught in another time, another place. For a second, he was damned sorry he had fallen behind the others when they'd spotted Schnell; when he had heard the unmistakable groans of someone in terrible pain.

He had found the source of those sounds. Of those animallike moans. Those pleas.

The room was some torture chamber. A hellhole for both the dead, and, incredibly, Walker discovered, the living.

The naked, blood-drenched bodies of native Congolese had been piled in a glass-enclosed shell at the back of the room. Specimen jars, human organs of every kind and shape floating in formaldehyde, lined the walls.

But it was the living that captured Walker's disbelief and growing sense of horror. Prisoners had been left strapped to metal tables, blood pumping from open chest cavities and lower bellies where organs had been removed. A feeble moan sounded from the lips of a woman.

Was this what they had found when the Allies had liberated Dachau, Auschwitz?

Walker unleashed his Atchisson on the living. The mercy shots brought the brothers Husseini and several Star of David commandos storming into the room. Horror and rage instantly masked the faces of Abraham and Ruben Husseini.

Walker grabbed an M15, pulled the grenade, rolled the bomb across the floor.

As Walker and the Star of David forces scattered down the gangway, a whooshing ball of fire boiled through the doorway from that hell-chamber. Debris rained down on the sea of black drums.

Seconds later, the Hangman, his Death Row soldiers, and the Star of David forces reunited on the gangway.

"What was that all about?" White growled at Walker.

Hangman smelled the roasting flesh, knew what was in the ruins of that burning room.

The look of cold, murderous fury had still not faded from the eyes of the Husseinis.

"The past, my friend," Ruben Husseini said, tight-lipped. "Hell from the past."

"White, Walker," Hangman said, "load up. Bring the ceiling down on those drums. Then seal up the mouth of every tunnel on your way out. I suggest you put on your masks, just in case."

As the Husseinis led their strike force out of the underground complex, White and Walker began loading HE projectiles into their MM-1s.

Hangman and his troops followed the Star of David strike force into the tunnel.

After they snugged on their gas masks, Walker and White unloaded HE rounds on the sea of drums. Dozens of the death containers sailed the crests of roaring explosions. The ex-Klansman and the ex-heavyweight turned the MM-1s toward the ceiling. A deafening salvo of HE detonations blasted off huge sections of rock. Tons of debris pounded down onto the drums. Volatilized liquid swirled into the air under the continuous barrage of explosions and descending rock slabs. Swastika banners slid from the walls and were buried quickly by rubble.

As the Hangman moved out of the cave into the flaming kill-zone that was the compound, he heard shots. He spotted brown-uniformed soldiers going down as Star of David commandos pumped bullets into their heads.

"Hey, there!" he yelled after the Husseinis. "Husseini! I want a prisoner, goddamnit. Assholes," he muttered under his breath, striding toward the devastated ruins.

Behind the Hangman, White and Walker moved out of the caves, reloading their MM-1s. Quickly, they sealed the mouth of each cave. The succession of thunderous explosions finally caved in the very bottom of the foothills, tons of dirt and rock avalanching, sealing the gruesome tomb, burying the deadly payload beyond.

And the Hangman got his prisoner.

Two commandos hauled Herbert Schnell out of the jungle. They tossed the Surgeon at the feet of the Husseinis. A commando kicked Schnell in the ribs, cursing.

Hangman hastened his strides toward the Surgeon. He saw the gung-ho, vengeance-crazed asshole place the barrel of his Uzi against Schnell's temple. A curse ripped from the Hangman's lips as he saw the commando's grip visibly tighten on the Uzi.

CHAPTER FIFTEEN

"Hold it!" the Hangman yelled, then squeezed off a quick burst from his Uzi, slugs drilling into the ground in front of the commando.

Everyone froze.

Ruben Husseini flashed the SOD man a startled look. Anger then hardened his dark eyes.

For long moments the towering walls of crackling fire engulfing the kill-zone broke the threatening silence. Delayed blasts ripped from the blackened hulls of the gunship *Luftwaffe*, pillars of thick, oily smoke spiraling skyward.

As he strode toward the commando who had forced Herbert Schnell to his knees, Hangman kept his finger wrapped tightly around the Uzi. "Seems to be the only way I can get you people to pay any attention to me around here," he growled at the Husseinis.

"You push your luck, my CIA friend," Abraham Husseini warned.

"Fuck you, Jack," Hangman rasped. "It may be

over for the Star of David, but we've still got to go
into South Africa. You copying?"

Heat shimmer rippled around the Death Row soldiers as they followed the specialist, the CIA kill-
team parting tongues of licking fire, weapons ready.

Hangman saw that Herbert Schnell was in bad
shape. A sliver of his monocle was embedded in his
eye. Blood poured down the SS man's face. He shook
violently as he looked up at the Hangman.

Hangman looked at the commando, who released
his hold on Schnell.

"He stumbled and fell on his face," the commando
explained.

I bet, pal, he thought. The conquerors had turned
vicious, damn right. *An eye for an eye makes everybody blind, huh?*

Hangman grabbed a handful of Schnell's hair.
The Nazi Surgeon cried out in pain as the SOD man
slid the piece of glass from his eye.

Someone called out to the Husseinis from the
gunships.

"Get up," the SOD man ordered the Surgeon as
his search-and-destroy team gathered around him.

"American . . ."

Hangman looked over to Ruben Husseini. He saw
two 155mm shells placed on the ground by commandos.

"Those gotta be the nukes," Walker rumbled.

"I would say that we escaped by the skin on our
teeth, wouldn't you?" Ruben Husseini said.

Hangman was thinking ahead. "Can any of your
people hook those one-fifty-fives up to our gunship?"

Husseini nodded. "It would take some time."

"How long?"

The elder Husseini shrugged. "Seven, eight
hours."

"Too long. We can't wait."

White chuckled. "What are you thinking about,
Cap'n? Blowing up Pretoria?"

Moments later, the whine of rotor blades pierced the air. Heads swung toward the southern fringes of the compound. Star of David commandos leveled Uzis and a couple of LAWs in that direction, too.

The skull and crossbones showed.

"Hold your goddamn fire!" Hangman barked. "That's ours." *Right on the damned money and not a second too late.* Time to get the hell out of there.

This war, he knew, was far from over for them.

"I'm taking this guy," Hangman told the Husseinis, hauling Herbert Schnell away from the airstrip. "I need some answers. And we can't be dicking around here."

"You just make sure the Nazi is returned," Ruben Husseini growled. "We will not go back to Israel with no evidence of our victory here. do you understand?"

"I'm reading you loud and clear, Jack," Hangman called back as Spectre landed.

As Hangman's troops boarded the gunship, the Husseinis strode across the compound. Hangman saw them coming, and they didn't look any happier than they did two seconds ago.

"Now what?"

"You get your answers and you return the Nazi immediately," Ruben Husseini said. "I don't think I made myself clear."

"Look, pal, I don't want to hold this asshole any longer than I have to. He's excess baggage, along for the fucking ride. When and where do you want him?"

"As soon as we strike against the diamond field and finish our mission here," Abraham Husseini said.

"That's exactly where we're headed. See you there. Or in Hell."

Hangman slung Schnell into the fuselage and climbed aboard. The pilot, his face hidden by a dark visor, turned and updated the Hangman. "Those choppers flew upriver. I chased them about ten klicks, then they set down on the other side."

"All seven?"

"Yeah."

"Get this bird airborne. Fly downriver. We're hitting the diamond field. Drop us off. Give us air-fire support, but choose your targets with extreme care. I don't need a bunch of pissed-off natives chasing us down because you got trigger-happy and blew away a few hundred Congolese." *And then have you tell me later, "Sorry, but they all look alike to me,"* Hangman thought.

"Roger."

As Spectre lifted off, Hangman went to work on Herbert Schnell, driving a fist into the Nazi's blinded eye. Sliding the Detonics .45 from his holster, he glimpsed his troops out of the corner of his eye. They took seats on the bench in silence. Lucien Schnell just stared at the floor, a distant look in his eyes. He didn't seem to even be aware that his infamous uncle was getting manhandled, blood streaming down his face. None of them appeared to give a shit what he did at the moment. All of them whipped, minds fucked, and they just wanted to catch their breath. Williams and White flicked Zippos, fired up smokes.

Hangman snatched Herbert Schnell by the front of his shirt and flung him to the floorboard. Rotor wash pounded the SOD man, and Schnell as the Nazi fell into the open doorway.

"Start talking, Jack. Names. Places. Who in South Africa is on the receiving end of your payload? And where?"

Hangman was primed to blow this guy's head off. They had walked away from that garrison without one hostage. And it suddenly looked as if he was on the Husseinis' shit list. More trouble, yeah. With no end in sight.

"I did not want this. I did not want this," Herbert

Schnell blurted, shaking his head, teeth clenched as he seemed to fight off waves of agony.

The guy was coming unglued pretty quick, the Hangman thought. Too quick. "It's a little late for all that, pal. By about fifty years. You've got two seconds to start talking."

"John Endicott...Maurice D-Denyvan...P-Petre Samon.... They are who you want.... They are our supporters.... They have financed the Fourth Reich—"

"Where are they?"

"Th-they are at the garrison...now...awaiting the shipment...the Transvaal...along the Botswana border."

"White, get a map and bring it here."

"There are maybe a hundred South African dissidents there."

"You mean terrorists, don't you?"

"*Ja.* Assassination squads. White and black. We have all the elements from every branch of the military and police on our side. Even Recces commandos."

Recces, he thought. Hell. Hold on a second here, pal. Looks like they'd be going up against commandos regarded worldwide as every bit as tough as the SAS, Green Berets, and the best shock troops the Israelis or West Germans had. The Recces were the toughest bastards in South Africa. Hit-and-run tactics that had their origins in the Anglo–Boer Wars. Hell, he finally thought, here they were, flying right into the eye of the Afrikaner hurricane. Staring right into the murderous eye of the Boer fury. Recces. And his six cutthroats weren't exactly the Green Berets.

But they were a war machine. Undisciplined, insolent, mutinous—all that. But they would kill the enemy. Damn near with glee. At the moment, though, as he looked at his troops, that machine was running low on fuel.

White spread the enlarged map of South Africa out beside Schnell.

"Point," the SOD man growled at Schnell. "And make it good. Because I just might be taking you along for the joyride."

With a shaking finger, Schnell indicated the area where the garrison was located.

"Mark it," he told White, then returned ice-eyed attention to the surviving camp *doktor* of Auschwitz. "Okay, so you're telling me all the big shitkickers are going to be there, right?"

"Nein."

"What the hell do you mean, *nein?*"

"There are many others...perhaps hundreds... spread over the Republic...but they are all waiting for Endicott's force at the garrison to make its move."

"In other words, they're just fair-weather shitkickers. All right, I'll buy that."

Hangman let out a breath. Spectre hadn't put any altitude on the Congo River. Flying low, nosedown, the warbird was screaming ahead, all battle systems set on standby. The glinting black surface of the river blurred past the Hangman, thirty feet below. Hangman started to consider what he should do with the Surgeon.

Damn, he could've used a one-fifty-five or two. It sure would've made life a little easier. Now they had to do it all the hard way. But then again...

Suddenly, something whooshed into the river below him. Water geysered, stinging his face. The intercom crackled with the pilot's voice.

"I've got four birds. Bearing down hard on our aft."

Hangman stuck his head out of the fuselage.

"What've you got there, Cap'n?" Mac White called out, his excited tone cutting clearly through the rotor whine.

What they had were four big warbirds flying under the swastika. Two hundred meters upriver, the Hangman saw the gunship formation. The *Luft-waffe* nearly skimmed the river's surface, spread out in a staggered line. Pros, yeah.

And rocket pods were already blazing.

Hangman hit the intercom button. "Put her into a hairpin, fly-boy, but give us thirty seconds first. Then open up with everything you've got!"

"Are you fucking nuts!" the pilot rasped. "We'll only get one shot at all four."

One shot, yeah, he knew. But it was their only chance. With four-to-one odds, they had better act quickly. *Blitzkrieg* quickly. Those warbirds would chase them down soon. One hit from any of those gunships, and they were looking at a watery grave. Looking out at the world from the belly of a crocodile.

Long odds. But one roll of the dice was all they would get anyway.

CHAPTER SIXTEEN

It was an emergency-action drill they had practiced aboard Spectre at least once a week. The Hangman was momentarily surprised, and pleased, at just how quickly his troops leapt into action. That pleasure was short-lived. It could be the last thing he ever felt.

Hangman hit the button beside the intercom. Three gun holes starboard and three more portside slid open. Instantly, Jackson and Schnell manned the Bofors cannons. Barnes took the 20mm.

Seconds earlier, the Hangman had told Spectre's two navigators to work their field of fire from left to right. He and Walker, toting the Armbrust crossbow antitank bazookas, would sweep the *Luftwaffe* from right to left.

Hangman checked his watch. Three seconds to spare.

"Let's do it there, Hannibal!" the specialist told Walker. Then, rope secured around his waist, he climbed out onto the mounted rocket pods, straddling the metallic death bin like a cowboy mounting a bareback bronco as White held onto the rope. Kneeling in the doorway, Williams holding back on the rope around his waist, Walker lifted the fourteen-pound Armbrust to his shoulder.

Spectre decelerated, went into a hairpin turn. The jungle tree line and black river surface meshed in Hangman's sight, blurring as he fought the tremendous pull of gravity, relying on White to keep him from pitching into the water. *If White had ever wanted to get rid of him* . . .

The *Luftwaffe* shot its load.

Spectre banked portside a millisecond before four volcanic sprays of water washed over the Hangman and his gun crew.

The Nazi gunships bore down—big, black metallic predatory birds of death swooping in for the kill.

Spectre steadied, hovered directly between the staggered *Luftwaffe* formations. Less than a hundred meters ahead of Spectre the Nazi warbirds began to slow, rotor blades whipping water needles across the river's black sun-shimmering surface.

Gunship showdown over the Congo River. He could have been Bat Masterson in another life, Hangman thought.

Hangman and Walker triggered the Armbrusts. Spectre unleashed a combined minigun and rocket barrage. Bofors boomed 40mm hell-bomb payloads.

And the Hangman's war machine struck their own V-2 paydirt.

As Spectre veered away from a line of tracking *Luftwaffe* fire, explosions pounding the river's surface, a tidal wave of water washing over the gunship, four tremendous fireballs thunderclapped in the distance. Rolling, fiery clouds poured over the river, wreckage screeching as warped hulls collided in the inferno. For a long moment, the blue sky seemed to turn white above the flashing blaze.

White let out a piercing Rebel yell. "John Wayne,

look out! Italian Stallion, fuck you! We got the real thing here! We got the fucking Captain!"

Yeah, flatter me, pal, the Hangman thought. *Then you'll try to flatten me.*

White grabbed the Hangman as he stood reaching for the edge of the fuselage doorway and hauled the specialist safely into the gunship.

"The diamond field next?" the pilot asked.

Hangman pushed the intercom button. "Nice shooting, pal. Think you're up to a repeat performance?"

"Fucking-A."

White let out another Rebel yell. "God, I love that kinda talk!"

Right away, the Hangman and his troops saw they were late for the slaughter. The diamond field was one sprawling hell-zone of insanity. It was obvious that the Israeli–West German commandos had gotten the better of the Fourth Reich here, having used the Nazis' own warbirds to make their *blitzkrieg.*

Already, the vultures had gathered in the sky. Thick, swirling black clouds of scavengers.

Watchtowers had been turned to pyres.

Countless brown-uniformed soldiers had gone down under the blazing miniguns of the gunships.

Liberated blacks ran amok, helping to turn the tide of battle completely to the side of the Star of David.

"There's your black revolution, champ," Mac White said to Walker as the Hangman and the other Death Row soldiers crowded into the doorway.

"Those guys didn't waste a second getting here," Williams commented.

Suddenly, autofire roared up at Spectre as a retreating group of Nazis cut loose on them.

Instantly, as lead hornets zinged off the gunship's hull, White plucked two MKs off his webbing and pulled the pins. As Spectre soared over the Nazis, the ex-Klansman dropped the frag grenades. Two saffron explosions ripped through the Hitlerians, shredding their numbers.

Hangman ordered the pilot to land. Near the western edge of the compound, Spectre touched down. Hangman saw that the tide of Fourth Reichers, forced to flee the overwhelming numbers, was being pushed toward them.

The war machine thundered on.

Belted M60s ripped open in the hands of Barnes and Schnell. Walker and White unleashed the MM-1s. Hangman, Jackson, and Williams cut loose with Uzis. Boiling fireclouds, a hell-storm of 9mm lead rained over the three dozen running Hitlerians. Bodies hurtled in every direction. Dust swirled, dismembered limbs cartwheeling skyward.

Still, a number of Nazis ran for the hills toward the east.

Quickly, the Hangman and his troops disembarked. Guns bucking, blazing, MM-1s coughing out fiery HE payloads, the war machine swept over the remaining Hitlerians within seconds.

Jubilant shouts thundered across the diamond field as hundreds of black workers surrounded the brothers Husseini and their commandos.

Hangman led his troops toward the Nazi-hunters. It was a long, tiresome walk halfway across the compound. But, he knew, they weren't home free. He had to keep that adrenaline rush going.

Ruben Husseini, Uzi by his side, walked up to greet the CIA strike force. He nodded thoughtfully, a smile fleeting over his lips.

"You guys do good work," Mac White commented, making a quick assessment of the vanquished enemy numbers.

Several vultures had descended on bodies strewn around the perimeter.

"It is over for us, my American friend," the elder

Husseini told Hangman. "I suspect you have gotten the information you needed from the Nazi?"

Hangman looked at Williams. "Go get him."

"It has been a good fight," Ruben Husseini said. "Unfortunately, I have lost many good men. More than half my force. But we were all prepared to give our lives here to accomplish this mission."

Abraham Husseini, a blood-soaked tourniquet wrapped around his thigh, limped up behind his brother.

Around the Hangman, excited Bantu chatter filled the air as blacks rounded up weapons, congratulating, thanking the Star of David commandos.

"Hey, Sarge!"

Hangman turned and looked back at the gunship. Williams walked away from the cloud of dust whirlpooling beneath the rotors.

"He's not there!"

Hangman cursed under his breath.

"What does this mean?" Ruben Husseini growled.

"It means we fucked up," the Hangman rasped, turning to run back toward the gunship.

"Hell, he couldn't have gotten too far," Hangman said, shouting at Ruben Husseini in order to be heard above the rotor scream as the SOD man and the Star of David commando leader stood in Spectre's doorway.

Together, they searched the marshy shoreline of the Congo River. Nothing but a few hippos stretched out in the mud, basking in the sun. And the Hangman was surprised at just how many crocodiles he saw resting in tangled reptilian clusters in the marshy areas.

Husseini had sent out the three pirated gunships with his own men to scour the jungle perimeter around the diamond field. Hangman checked his Seiko. 1400. He wanted to wrap this up and get the hell on down to the Transvaal. He wanted a piece of that Boer fury.

Finally, the pilot banked Spectre, turned around, and headed the gunship back downriver.

Surprisingly enough, Hangman thought, Husseini hadn't lit into him about the Nazi's escape. But then again, he thought, maybe he was throwing off some pretty ugly vibes to the leader of the Jewish commandos. Both of them, he knew, were strung out, walking a dangerously nerve-frayed tightrope. They were about one word away from bare-knuckle city.

"There!" Husseini shouted, pointing.

Hangman spotted Herbert Schnell a moment later. The last surviving Nazi of Auschwitz was a good fifty yards out into the water, swimming like hell for the other side. A last desperate bid for freedom. And a suicide run, the Hangman saw moments later as he spotted something else in the river besides Schnell. He reached for the intercom, but the pilot's voice came on first.

"I see him. I'll take her down."

Quickly, the Hangman threw a rope ladder out of the fuselage. Hangman's soldiers crowded into the doorway.

They saw the crocodiles, sleek dark shapes knifing through the river's surface. Long snouts rearing up out of the water. Jaws opening.

Spectre lowered, descending on top of Schnell. Rotor wash sprayed water needles up into the Hangman's face as he shouted, "Schnell! Grab the ladder!"

The Nazi Surgeon took another stroke and then looked up the ladder as it was lowered toward him. He hesitated as if deciding whether to keep swimming or grab the ladder.

The decision was made for Schnell.

As the gunship continued to lower, the Hangman saw the inevitable. Schnell's scream was bone-chilling but short. The Surgeon lurched, thrashing beneath the surface. Hangman saw gaping jaws open, jagged cone-shaped teeth flashing for a second, as six giant amphibians tore into the Nazi, dragging him under. Schnell's head poked through the surface, his mouth vented. A split second later, a bloody maw broke through the surface. Massive jaws clamped down over the Surgeon's face.

Hangman heard Husseini mutter a curse. But Husseini didn't want Schnell bad enough to dive into that churning hell-zone after him.

None of them did.

The Hangman turned, momentarily searching the haunted faces of his troops.

Lucien Schnell walked back to the bench. Like a wooden soldier.

The Hangman stood in the open doorway of Spectre. He drew deep on his Camel, staring out at the long, deep shadows that blanketed the high plains country of Zambia.

Sunset.

Sixty feet below, the Zambezi River blurred past him. A dangerous, circuitous route along the Zambian–Zimbabwean border, yeah. But Spectre had thrown up its radar-jamming screen. And they weren't slowing down for anything. Not even for a whole fleet of fucking MIGs.

About an hour ago, though, the pilot had warned him that he'd picked something up on radar. Three somethings. By their rate of movement on radar, the pilot judged the objects on his screen to be helicopters.

Hell, he thought, since leaving the kill-zone in Zaire, everything had gone along without a hitch. Maybe too smoothly. That was the hitch.

Several hours ago they had refueled at the main Fourth Reich garrison up the Congo River. They had reloaded the rocket pods, attached two TOWs to the portside skids, and told the Husseinis to kiss their ass.

They were going in for one final mop-up.

He hoped. Damn, he was tired.

They had just enough fuel to reach the mission supply site beyond Victoria Falls. Beyond that, the rest of the operation was up for grabs. He had no recon on the Boer hardsite in the Transvaal.

And virtually no idea what in Hell they were faced with next.

CHAPTER SEVENTEEN

Under the cover of night, Spectre crossed the Botswana border into the Transvaal, lights off. Black greasepaint on their faces, Williams and White flanked the Hangman in the windswept doorway. Barnes, toting an M60, belted shells criss-crossing his chest like a bandolier, was going in with the ground troops, too. White's MM-1 was loaded, and the ex-Klansman, as usual, looked every bit as kill-hungry as any of the other six.

A black, barren plain stretched away from the gunship—the farthest southeastern outer fringes, Hangman knew, of the Kalahari Desert. According to the intel he'd forced out of Herbert Schnell, the Fourth Reich headshed was just twenty kilometers ahead.

Hangman felt the adrenaline rush. This airborne Viking vessel, he knew, was bound for its final Operation Apocalypse destination. Next stop: Who knows?

It could all end here, on a sun-sucked, hellish

landscape, he knew. But his war machine was fueled up on adrenaline and kill-lust, ready to roll. The end would come hard for all of them.

And Spectre's pilots were every bit as itchy, he sensed, to deliver the final payload to the new Reich. Hell, he didn't know the first thing about the gunship's two CIA-chosen navigators, but he had to give them a lot of credit. They knew what they were doing.

Still, the waiting was stretching everyone's nerves to a snapping point.

Minutes later, a chain of black hills came into sight to the south. Spectre gained some altitude, and the Hangman saw the lights of the compound in the distance.

The hardsite?

The intercom crackled with the pilot's voice. "Just got a call over the radio. Or, I should say, a warning. Guy wants to know the password. I told him we're bringing in the shipment, but he still says he needs the password first."

Damn. Hangman looked at his troops and dryly remarked, "How come you guys let me forget to ask about that?"

A few "go to Hell" looks told him he was barking up the wrong tree.

"Set her down," Hangman told the pilot. "Sounds like we've found the right place."

Moments later, Spectre landed at the foot of the hills. Hangman, White, Williams, and Barnes disembarked. Swiftly, the four-man slaughter force moved up the hills in a staggered formation.

A deep blackness swallowed the Hangman and his troops. But, within moments, there would be enough firelight to guide them into the bowels of Hell. He hoped.

Spectre lifted off to deliver its cargo of annihilation from above. Hangman believed that they could catch the bulk of the South African dissident force asleep. Provided, of course, someone monitoring the radar didn't sound the alarm.

Two dark shapes appeared at the top of the hill. One guy opened up with an assault rifle. The other guy hollered something.

Dumbass, Hangman thought, his team instantly alerted to the sudden danger, pinpointing the voice right away with a lead "Hello" as a cacophony of automatic-weapons fire erased those two shadows from the hill's crest.

Topping the hill, the Hangman signaled his team to spread out. They charged down the hill into the compound as Spectre launched its TOW missiles.

Soldiers bolted from bivouacs, firing wildly at the black deathbird. Two ear-shattering HE detonations blew large numbers back into the sleep of forever. Rockets whooshed away from Spectre's pods, unearthing a long row of quarters. Explosions pulped Land Rovers and armored assault vans used by the South African police and military.

Yeah, the Hangman thought, leading the Charge of his Death Row Brigade, they'd found the right place, all right.

Spectre's *blitzkrieg* split the night asunder. From the fuselage, Walker raked the compound with the MM-1. Shouts from running figures became screams as a half-dozen blasts turned night into temporary day with blinding saffron flashes. Jackson and Schnell, manning the Bofors 40mm cannons, pulped the sandbagged antiaircraft area with a thunderous barrage.

The Hangman and his troops moved into a hellzone of utter and awesome destruction. Walls of fire roared up into the night. Guys were running in all directions, shooting at the sky, raking the shadows with R-4s. Five German gunships felt the wrath of Spectre's *blitzkrieg* and the combined MM-1–Bofors barrage. Gunship wreckage vomited across the compound on searing mushroom fireballs. Explosions hurtled three deuce-and-a-half trucks into the sky.

One leg draped over the edge of the doorway, Walker began to reload the MM-1. R-4s barked, pencil flames marking the compound grounds like beacons. A 5.56mm slug tore through Walker's shoulder. He yelped in pain, flinching away as slugs tattooed the hull.

Spectre banked to east, flying back in for another strafing kill.

Hangman and his war machine rolled into the hell-zone. White's MM-1 vaporized a concentrated group of enemy numbers, launching bodies skyward like bowling pins.

Barnes cut loose with the M60, big, hot lead tumblers mowing down would-be Fourth Reichers.

Hangman opened up with his Uzi, stitching five shadows as slugs drilled into the ground around him. Veering away from his soldiers, he ran toward what he thought was the command post. He had a gut feeling about that place.

He was looking for three conspirators. Three pieces of slime.

Overhead, the SOD man heard the roar of Spectre's miniguns. Beside him, the din of SMG fire pierced into his eardrums. Ahead, he saw shadows corkscrewing to the ground. This was a fucking massacre, he knew. But that's what he'd hoped for. Get in. Get the job done. Get the hell out.

As he neared the headshed, the front door burst open. A tall guy in a brown uniform stepped into the doorway. Hangman saw the R-4 in the guy's hands swing his way, a short burst barking from the South African assault rifle.

But a quicker, longer burst from the Hangman's Uzi sent that soldier on a one-way ride.

Combat senses electrified on adrenaline overdrive, the Hangman flung himself against the wall beside the headshed's front doorway. He peered inside. Nothing. He squeezed off a quick burst, expended his magazine. Quickly, he rammed home a fresh thirty-two round clip. Barging through the doorway, he found what he had come for.

Three guys. Not soldiers, hell no. They were cringing in the far corner of the Spartanly furnished room. And he hadn't seen flashier threads since he'd begun this kill-hunt in the ghetto of Detroit.

Three white Super Flies. Shaking like they were wired to electrodes. Hell, he would've sworn he saw a yellow streak go down the back of their pants.

"Endicott?"

A nod from one of the dudes.

"Denyvan?"

Another nod.

"Samon?"

Yeah, he had all the nuts right there in one shell. All the garbage in one trashcan.

"Wh-who are you?"

Hangman showed these three parasites his best graveyard smile. "Jesus."

And he emptied the whole fucking magazine into those guys.

He made that Uzi sing.

Parabellum slugs keep falling on my head.

Slapping a fresh mag into the Uzi, the Hangman turned. As he headed through the doorway, a fist crashed into his jaw. Stars danced in front of his eyes as he reeled to the ground, Uzi flying from his grasp. Looking up, he saw one big black sonofabitch moving toward him. A Zulu. Not somebody to be bullshitting around with, he knew. And there was blood on that Zulu warrior from head to toe. Lots of blood. Shrapnel had shredded the uniform right off the black warrior's back. And the rage of Hell was burning in that guy's eyes.

Hangman leapt to his feet. He cycloned into a reverse spinning kick, the heel of his boot cracking on the Zulu's jaw. The Zulu stumbled sideways and almost pitched to the ground. Almost.

The sonofabitch had a jaw like granite, the Hangman thought. And, before he could reach for his Detonics or his commando knife, the Zulu came at him. A rampaging bull with fists flailing. The Hangman took a right, then a left that dropped him on his back. Somehow he kept his senses, using the momentum of his fall and throwing himself into a reverse somersault. For a split second, his legs felt like jelly as he stood, squaring off with the Zulu.

Explosions ripped the night around the SOD man and the Zulu. Wavering mountains of fire lit the savage intensity on each man's face.

The Zulu feinted with a left, threw a right roundhouse. Hangman ducked the brute force of the blow and felt the Zulu's knuckles hammer off the top of his head.

But the guy had just thrown his best punch and missed. Hangman countered instantly, pile-driving the toe of his boot deep into the Zulu's gut. As the Zulu doubled over, the SOD man drove his knee up into his deadly adversary's face, felt nose bone crunch like Styrofoam.

"Havin' a little trouble there, Sarge?" he heard Williams yell from somewhere.

As the Zulu's head snapped up from the knee kick, Hangman hammered a right off the black warrior's jaw, then whiplashed the same fist back across cheekbone. Incredibly, the Zulu held onto consciousness and exploded a straight right off the Hangman's right eye.

"Hey, Sarge, you sure you don't need no help there?"

Staggering back, the Hangman saw the Zulu charge him through blurry vision. He had one shot. At survival. And that was it.

Hangman waited, timed the kick perfectly. The toe of his right boot speared into the side of the Zulu's knee, shattering bone. As the Zulu crumpled to his one good knee, his hand snaked out. Hangman twisted his body, felt the hand claw into the top of his left thigh where his balls had been a split second ago. With rage and fear-powered might, Hangman lanced the end of his elbow into the Zulu's temple.

A sickening crack of bone.

The Zulu thudded to the ground.

Shoulders sagging, the Hangman stood over the fallen Zulu, catching his breath.

He didn't think he'd ever feel so relieved to see somebody dead again. Tomorrow he'd be feeling the price for this lethal encounter. His head felt as if it had been split open with the sharp edge of a shovel. Repeatedly, he spat out large streams of blood.

He saw Williams, White, and Barnes running toward him. Groggily, Hangman picked up his Uzi.

Spectre soared in from the south and landed.

Dust blew over the Hangman. The stench of blood and charred flesh burned his senses. He seemed to be looking out at the world, pinned to a roulette wheel. Williams, forever the asshole, had the balls to laugh.

"You gonna be all right there, Sarge?"

Hangman pushed past his troops and led them toward Spectre.

Dead men were strewn all over the kill-zone.

Flaming wreckage littered the compound and its perimeter.

They had done a hell of a job, he knew.

It was time to take it on home.

But first he had some unfinished business with the Husseinis.

It regarded the spoils of war.

After this one, the Hangman thought, these guys deserved a little bonus.

And he was including himself in for a piece of that action.

EPILOGUE

Dawn broke over Zaire as Spectre approached the ruins of the Nazi outpost. There, the Israeli–German commandos were gathering in large burlap sacks and crates.

Hangman, his chin resting on his shoulder, sitting beneath the intercom, heard the pilot's voice through a pulsing buzz in his head. Something about the Jewish commandos. Something about an LZ. He opened one eye and looked out at a world that would have been ugly even if he'd been sitting in some L.A. penthouse with about six blond vixens fixing to—

The hell with it.

As pummeled as he felt, he knew his troops weren't exactly going to jump for fucking joy, either. Particularly when he told them about their cut in pay.

Damn, his head felt as if it were swollen twice its size. He was hungry, tired, beat to shit. And on this morning, he was looking out at that ugly world through only one good eye. The other eye was swollen shut.

His cutthroats, he noticed, were either asleep or half-asleep.

Hangman braced his back against the wall and stood. Damn, he could have used a cold beer. Or a special speaking engagement at the UN, he thought. Or maybe a guest appearance at a National Security Council meeting. Yeah, he'd walk in there...

Ah, the hell with it.

"What's up, Sarge?"

Hangman waited as Spectre touched down near the Star of David commandos. "Go back to sleep," he told Williams. "You need your ugly rest."

That crack almost made him feel good.

As the Hangman hopped out of Spectre, the brothers Husseini broke away from their group.

Hangman had his eye on the pile of burlap sacks and crates.

He wasn't going to take no for an answer. What he was going to do if he heard no, he wasn't exactly sure.

"My American friend."

Christ, this guy was all light and warmth and syrupy sweetness. The shithead. What the hell?

It made him want to puke.

"I take it the remainder of your mission was a success?"

"You could say that."

"It looks as if you paid quite a price for that success," Ruben Husseini commented.

And the Hangman wanted to wipe the smile right off that guy's face.

Hangman looked toward the confiscated treasure. Behind the SOD man, the Death Row soldiers had crowded into Spectre's doorway.

Husseini looked back at the treasure, too.

"Who's claiming the spoils of war?" Hangman asked in a gravelly voice.

Ruben Husseini's smile remained easy. "It will go back to Israel. Perhaps it will be used to help finance future operations for our strike force."

"Yeah, perhaps." Hangman paused, searching both faces of the fighting brothers for a moment. He jerked a thumb over his shoulder. "You wouldn't mind giving those guys about five minutes to help themselves, would you?"

Ruben Husseini's easy expression melted. He looked deeply into the Hangman's eyes for a stretched second. Finally, Husseini's gaze faltered. He smiled, shrugged. "No one has made an official claim yet. And you and your men have been an invaluable help. No one would object."

Hangman turned toward his cutthroats. "Clear out one of those weapons crates."

He'd never seen six happier fuckers in all of his life. Hell, he'd never seen six guys move so fast.

"Hey!" he shouted. His soldiers froze in the doorway. "Let's not plan on making a habit of this."

He got a thumbs-up. A couple of laughs.

Yeah, pillage, babe, pillage. A little pillaging would be good for their black souls.

Then let's take it on home.

He wanted twenty-four hours of shut-eye.

A full bottle from the top shelf.

And a carton of Camels. Unfiltered.

The simple things in life, yeah.

KILLSQUAD

by Frank Garrett

WANTED: A world strike force—the last hope of the free world—the ultimate solution to global terrorism!

THE WEAPON: Six desperate and deadly inmates from Death Row led by the invincible Hangman...

THE MISSION: To brutally destroy the terrorist spectre wherever and whenever it may appear...

KILLSQUAD #1 Counter Attack   75151-8/$2.50 US/$2.95 Can
America's most lethal killing machine unleashes its master plan to subdue the terrorquake planned by a maniacal extremist.

KILLSQUAD #2 Mission Revenge   75152-6/$2.50 US/$2.95 Can
A mad zealot and his army of drug-crazed acolytes are on the march against America...until they face the Killsquad—dealing an unholy apocalypse of its own!

KILLSQUAD #3 Lethal Assault   75153-4/$2.50 US/$3.50 Can
The Fourth Reich is rising again, until the Hangman rounds up his Death Row soldiers for some hard-nosed Nazi-hunting.

and coming soon

KILLSQUAD #4 The Judas Soldiers

75154-2/$2.50 US/$3.50 Can

A madman seeks to bring America to its knees with mass doses of viral horror, but Killsquad shows up with its own bloody cure.

Buy these books at your local bookstore or use this coupon for ordering:

Avon Books, Dept BP, Box 767, Rte 2, Dresden, TN 38225

Please send me the book(s) I have checked above. I am enclosing $_____
(please add $1.00 to cover postage and handling for each book ordered to a maximum of three dollars). Send check or money order—no cash or C.O.D.'s please. Prices and numbers are subject to change without notice. Please allow six to eight weeks for delivery.

Name _____

Address _____

City _____ State/Zip _____

Killsquad 12/86

VIETNAM

NOVELS WRITTEN BY
MEN WHO WERE THERE

THE BIG V William Pelfrey   67074-7/$2.95
"An excellent novel...Mr. Pelfrey, who spent a year as an
infantryman in Vietnam, recreates that experience with an intimacy
that makes the difference."
The New York Times Book Review

WAR GAMES James Park Sloan   01609-5/$3.50
Amidst the fierce madness in Vietnam, a young man searches for the
inspiration to write the "definitive war novel." "May become the new
Catch 22." *Library Journal*

AMERICAN BOYS Steven Phillip Smith 67934-5/$3.95 US/$4.95 Can
Four boys come to Vietnam for separate reasons, but each must
come to terms with what men are and what it takes to face dying. "The
best novel I've come across on the war in Vietnam." Norman Mailer

THE BARKING DEER Jonathan Rubin   61135-X/$3.50
A team of twelve men is sent to a Montagnard village in the central
highlands where the innocent tribesmen become victims of their
would-be defenders. "Powerful." *The New York Times Book Review*

COOKS AND BAKERS Robert A. Anderson   79590-6/$2.95
A young marine lieutenant arrives just when the Vietnam War is at its
height and becomes caught up in the personal struggle between the
courage needed for killing and the shame of killing. An Avon Original.
"A tough-minded unblinking report from hell." *Penthouse*

A FEW GOOD MEN Tom Suddick   01866-7/$2.95
Seven marines in a reconnaissance unit tell their individual stories
in a novel that strips away the illusions of heroism in a savage and
insane war. An Avon Original. "The brutal power of defined anger."
Publishers Weekly

AVON Paperbacks

Buy these books at your local bookstore or use this coupon for ordering:

Avon Books, Dept BP, Box 767, Rte 2, Dresden, TN 38225
Please send me the book(s) I have checked above. I am enclosing $_____
(please add $1.00 to cover postage and handling for each book ordered to a maximum of
three dollars). Send check or money order—no cash or C.O.D.'s please. Prices and numbers
are subject to change without notice. Please allow six to eight weeks for delivery.

Name _____

Address _____

City _____ State/Zip _____

Vietnam 6-86A